I0743531

RECKLESS WITH THE ROCKSTAR

A Mile High Rocked Novel

CHRISTINA HOVLAND

This book is a work of fiction. Names, characters, places, and incidents are the product of the author's imagination or are used fictitiously. Any resemblance to actual events, locales, or persons, living or dead, is coincidental.

For rights information, please contact:
Prospect Agency
551 Valley Road, PMB 377
Upper Montclair, NJ 07043
(718) 788-3217

Holly Ingraham, Development Editor
Audrey Nelson, Copy Editor
Shasta Schafer, Final Proofreader
Beth Carbutt, Editorial Goddess

Cover Model Photography by:
Lindee Robinson Photography
Cover Model: Daniel Smith

Everybody deserves to have a cheerleader in their corner who is willing to tell them,
"Oh honey, no."
And then gets right into the muck of it all to help fix what's wrong and show them why they started this journey to begin with.

For me, that's Holly Ingraham.

Make no mistake, this book is awesome because of her. I am forever grateful for all she did to help me bring Mach and Darla to life. Without Holly there would be no clarinets in this story, and there would be a whole lot more chickpea puffs. IFYKYK

So, yeah, this book is totally dedicated to Holly.

———————————

Prologue
MACH

———————————

MACH POWERS' life was a fucking fiasco.

Here's the deal. He was the ride-or-die friend everybody needs—always there to support his crew. And the fact that they'd do anything for him? Well, that just showed off more of his awesomeness.

Yeah, Mach adored his makeshift family of friends. He'd adore them more if his head wasn't about to explode from staring at the Nocturnal Cupid dating app.

Man, he really should've checked with his publicist before he decided to take things in his own hands and deflect attention away from his best bud, and brother from another mother, Tanner (and his girl Sami Jo). They'd found themselves in a pickle of a spotlight, and they needed someone to create a distraction. Mach took it upon himself to provide that for them.

He'd come up with the Nocturnal Cupid date all by himself. Which meant he had no one else to blame for his stupidity.

See, Mach had an idea and, honestly, he didn't even know how it came to him. The fact was that he did, and then he rolled with it. That idea being that he'd run a little publicity-generating contest for a date with… him.

This wasn't to really find a date—c'mon, he could do that on his own. He played guitar for Dimefront and he looked half-decent with good hair.

The set-up? The thousandth woman to swipe right on his profile won the contest. She'd get a date with Mach.

The tabloids ate it up like it was tacos on Tuesday.

He figured he wouldn't have to go through with it since there'd only be a few hundred entries. Everybody would win—he'd take the spotlight off Tanner and Sami Jo and there wouldn't be any collateral damage.

But surprise, surprise, he was wrong.

Turns out thousands of women were dying to go on this date with him. How the hell was he supposed to pick just one winner?

The entries. Dear God, the entries. Fuck, they kept pouring in, and the app shuffled them around so much, he couldn't tell who lucky number 1,000 was supposed to be.

Like trying to find a needle in a haystack, but with tons of single girls on an app instead of hay.

Yeah, that's how he found himself waiting to go on stage at Brek's Bar and sorting through online dating profiles. He and the other guys hung in the employee lounge—a small room with a Formica table, small sofa, crates stacked against the wall, and a fridge.

They often took the stage at Brek's when they came home to Denver, so this wasn't anything new. And, usually, this was the time he'd be amping himself up for the concert. But tonight he couldn't focus on anything except trying to solve this fucking puzzle. That's why he only half-listened to his buddies while they shot the shit.

"You can always help Mach figure out what the fuck he's doing," Bax said.

Mach glanced up at the mention of his name.

Bax was their lead singer and he lounged in his chair next to Linx, the bass player.

"I will let you handle the whole damn thing," Mach assured, poking away at his cell but, dammit, the entries shuffled again. Shit.

He clenched his jaw, ready to throw the whole situation out the window.

His friends all had time to balance their chairs on two legs in some kind of fucked-up contest with each other, and there he was still sorting his mess.

"Dealing with your dating profile sounds like the worst possible way to start feeling better about shit," Tanner said.

"Yeah, I can see that," Mach said, nodding, exasperated, and still poking at the screen.

Fu-u-uck, it shuffled again!

"Let me do it." Band publicist Courtney held out her hand. "And guys, put your chairs down. We don't need a cracked skull before the show, 'k?"

"You want to pick the winner?" Mach asked, frowning.

He should've asked her about the contest from the jump, because she would've had a way better plan. Actually, she *did* have a better plan and her plan actually worked.

He should hand her the phone. But he wasn't going to do that because if he handed *her* the phone, she'd actually try to pick someone he might be interested in. Or worse, someone actually interested in more than a one-off date with a musician.

He shivered because he was a lone wolf, and he didn't want to catch feelings.

"I'll go through and figure out the thousandth." Courtney made a gimme motion with her fingers.

"No." Mach shook his head. "Because you'll try to find

someone perfect for me. Not do it the math way. I don't want someone perfect for me, I prefer the math way, so she'll be horrible."

Courtney rolled her eyes. "Whatever."

"Time to hit the stage," their band manager Hans said, striding into the room.

"Hans could pick the thousandth," Courtney said. "He doesn't care who you match with. There will be no strategy at all."

"Are you still fighting with that?" Hans held out his hand. "Give me the phone."

Hans was the type of person you didn't ignore. Which meant that Mach didn't have a choice, so he handed over the cell.

Hans didn't even glance at the screen as he clicked the matched button. "Whoever that was? That's the thousandth. Deal with it." He tossed the phone back to Mach.

Mach caught the cell. Then he stared at the screen, straight-up shook. The cute blonde with bangs and the sweet smile made him pause. Her heart-shaped mouth had him grinning right along with her as he scanned her profile.

What do you do? Emergency Room Nurse
What makes you different? I stay calm in the middle of chaos.
Perfect Date? Netflix marathon with Chinese takeout
Yeah, hello… Darla Davis.

Chapter One
DARLA

DARLA DAVIS WAS BACK in the dating game and ready to give love a second…or third…chance. Who was counting at this point? She licked her lips and let out a long sigh because it'd been ages since she actually went on a date with somebody other than her fiancé. Ex-fiancé, actually. And, really, they didn't date much in the last few years. He was a super busy orthopedic surgeon. A big deal, and all that.

This guy tonight checked a lot of her boxes. Musician, check—she was so done with academics. Handsome— check, check. And he had tickets to see Dimefront at Brek's Bar—check, check, check.

Dimefront wasn't really her band of choice, but she understood why people liked them. And she figured maybe she should re-evaluate her taste in music as she re-evaluated her taste in men. This was a whole new life for her. A huge step.

Darla paused briefly to take in the people with all the cameras milling about outside the bar. There were over a dozen of them with their eyes trained on the door. Trained on her.

Paparazzi.

She did an internal eye roll.

Of course, they'd be watching the door. It was a big deal when Dimefront played. You didn't know which celebrities would show up.

Oh, what if it was that Dr. Phoenix Stone? Wouldn't that be fun?

Sure, she was off of dating doctors for forever, but he was the one hall pass she'd allow. The only one. And, if he were here, and she and her date didn't click, then at least she'd have a good view.

A little bubble of laughter rose up inside her on that thought, but she swallowed it down as she said, "Darla Davis. I should be on the list?"

The bulky bouncer with tattoos winding up his muscled neck grinned wide.

"Hey, Darla Davis," he said in a seriously deep baritone. "Have a good time."

Then he opened the door to let her inside.

The photographers snapped away, taking *her* photo as she started to step through the door. Huh? She wasn't exactly hot stuff.

She was a nurse. Nurses didn't have random photographers snapping their photos.

But if they wanted to take her photo, what the hell? She did a pose and wave like this was a red carpet and she was a starlet.

One last wave and she stepped through the door only a little late.

Honestly, at one point today she thought she'd have to cancel thanks to the stomach bug taking out half of

Denver. The emergency room was short staffed, and she got called in. *Whatchagonnado?*

She slipped her scarf down her neck and shook out her hair. The pink scarf with purple beads was one of her favorites, and something she rarely got to wear since, until recently, she didn't get the chance to go out that often. A quick look around the bar and…well…a bar was a bar, right? Dim and dark with neon beer signs and a jukebox in the back corner. An old school jukebox that probably still took loose change. The whole place smelled like stale beer, a mash-up of cologne, and sweat.

A man brushed against her as he slipped by to go outside. She side-stepped out of his way, still scanning the tables for her date. Maybe a little part of her was hoping for a glimpse of Dr. Stone.

No celebrity doctor in the house, but, honestly? This place was kind of perfect. The type of joint she'd never have been able to get her ex to visit.

And then she saw the guy from the app. Sitting in a corner booth, nursing his beer, and talking to the petite waitress. Darla recognized him from his profile picture on Nocturnal Cupid, but it didn't really do him justice. His eyes sparked full of humor in the dim light of the bar. The corners of his full lips crinkled when he smiled, and Darla found herself feeling actually hopeful. Heck, the little dimples at the edge of his lips that just barely kissed the edge of his close-trimmed beard practically smacked her in the face with a whole handful of hope.

Maybe the dating pool wasn't such a bad place to go swimming after all, because this guy was the stuff of wet dreams.

She'd only had enough time to change her clothes, slather on a bit of lipstick, and finger-comb her hair. Looking at him? She wished she'd taken some extra time with the makeup and the mirror. Could someone like her really handle a man like him?

Well, she was ready to give it a go.

God, he was attractive with eyes so blue every woman on the planet would probably discover a new love of sapphires if he looked their way. Not the lab-grown ones, either. The real freaking deal.

He'd gone with a T-shirt under his jacket with the jeans. The tee pulled taut against his muscles. The jeans? They were a sonnet waiting to be written.

Hell, had the man been a Cheeto, he'd have been the flaming hot variety.

His oddly attractive lopsided grin somehow actually complemented his leather jacket. His black hair was shaved at the sides with the top slicked back. The beard definitely upped his hot guy quotient. The intricate tattoo that peeked out from the edge of his jacket sleeve and wound around his wrist was an excellent final touch to the whole bad boy schtick he had going on.

The server slipped Mach a small piece of paper Darla didn't have to be a psychic to know held her digits.

Did he shove it in his pocket? Oh, hell, yes, he did. Her lips pursed all on their own without any direction from her brain.

But, actually, that was fine. It's not like they even knew each other, and the date hadn't officially started so he was under no obligation to her. Still, that didn't sit right, and the feeling in her belly sort of felt like the stomach bug she'd dealt with all day at the hospital.

But, hey, she could leave at any point. There was no reason she had to stay past the introductions. On this reasoning, Darla slowly made her way through the crowd, dodging drinks in hands, and skirting around the people surrounding the stage, all the way to the booth.

She brushed her bangs out of her eyes, and heaved a huge breath.

"Mach?" she asked.

Mach was such a great name. Sturdy and strong. She'd liked his name right away and it was part of the reason she swiped right. The way he spelled it differently, Mach, was so unique. Different was what she was going for this time when she got involved with anyone.

He glanced up from chatting with the server. The server who blinked extra hard and scanned Darla from head to toe. Then she smiled as though Darla was no competition at all. Two feet tall and made of stained glass… that's how Darla really felt inside. But she squared her shoulders, and she wouldn't show it.

Also, okay, so Darla might not have been the prize of all prizes, but she wasn't *ugh* either. So she could do without that extra helping of server side-eye.

"Darla," he said, unfolding himself from the booth. Gah, he was taller than she'd expected.

The bar had gone weirdly quiet, so only the music from the jukebox played in the background. What was that all about?

Darla didn't like the prickly sensation tingling the nerves along her spine.

Mach gestured for her to come closer, but Darla hesitated.

Then with confidence she totally faked, she closed the distance between them. But when she turned to slide onto the bench, the whole bar—every single person—was staring at her.

Mach seemed oblivious to the sudden silence, though, or the eyes on them.

"Lucky winner, Darla," he said, then he gestured to the server. "Anything she wants."

Lucky winner? A bit presumptuous, wasn't he? But, you know, confidence was a good thing in a dude.

"Club soda with a twist of lemon, please," she said.

"Anything else?" The server—her name tag read Pam—lifted her eyebrows almost as though suggesting Darla pick something else.

Darla's smile faltered a little, but she recovered. "That's it."

She wanted a clear head for this evening so she could appropriately determine compatibility. Vodka did not a clear head make.

They got settled—her on one side, him on the other. He stared at her funny, like he was waiting for her to say something.

"What do you think of Dimefront?" she asked, breaking the tab on small talk that didn't have to do with the rainy weather they'd had in Denver lately. "I was really surprised you could get us in here. These things are impossible to get tickets to."

He lifted one eyebrow in that way that people did that required superior forehead muscle control. Honestly, she didn't quite understand how they did it. She'd tried and never could make it work—always looked like she was about to have a stroke or something.

Then he cracked a broad smile. "Ha. Funny. Good one."

"What do you mean?" she asked, confused.

He stopped, his lips parting in surprise. "Do I *like* Dimefront?"

She nodded. That was the question. Small talk and all that.

His mouth opened a little, then closed, then opened again before he said, "Well… hell yeah. Sick beats and I understand the guitar player's pretty good." He paused. "What do you think?"

"I think their music is good," she said. "On the one hand, the unique lyrics make a person feel something different, you know? The heavy beats and overused chords definitely sound good, and the commercial appeal is undeniable."

He seemed to choke on his beer.

"You okay?" she asked.

"Go on," he sort of coughed out. "This is interesting."

"On the other hand, Dimefront music isn't quite up to the standards I grew up with. My parents were all into jazz and I have always been more into Miles Davis and Etta James, some Sinatra. You know, the greats."

He covered his mouth with his hand more and more as she spoke, like he was preventing himself from adding to the conversation.

Drat, she didn't mean to offend him. Of course, he liked Dimefront! This is where he brought her.

"It's okay if you don't like jazz," she assured, talking with her hands like she did when she got nervous. "I'm going through something of a transition in my life so I'm totally open to giving bands like Dimefront another shot. That's why I'm so stoked to be here with you."

"Bands like Dimefront?"

"Uh-huh. You know, the ones that are more for commercial purposes than love of the music."

"Uh…" He ducked his head, his eyes going wider. "You aren't joking?"

She gave a quick headshake. Was it getting hotter in there? It sure felt like it was. "Honesty is the best policy, right? Especially on the first date."

He stilled and went extra quiet.

"Am I missing something?" she asked.

He pointed to his chest. "I *play* for Dimefront. Guitar."

Darla's entire world zipped to a stop.

Ohhh, damn. Operation insertion of foot into mouth: complete.

Mach was not like a super cool alternative way to spell Mark, but like the airplanes that went wicked fast… and a rockstar name.

A tickle of a memory about a guitar player itched at her brain. No, was he a drummer? Something about a musician setting up a publicity date… gah, when had she read that? All the days melted together, it seemed, when a girl was in the midst of a life catastrophe, the implosion of her relationship, and two different strains of gastroenteritis right on top of each other.

But just like that, all the dominoes fell into place.

"Am I on a publicity stunt date?" she asked, slower than entirely necessary. "With… you?"

That would explain the pictures and everyone staring and… *oh, dear God.*

A furrow likely formed with the intensity that her eyebrows fell smack together. She rarely allowed that to happen because it'd eventually leave lines, and if she had lines she wanted them to be laugh lines. Not *what-the-fuck* lines.

He took a sip of his beer, then nodded. "Yeah. I, uh, sorta thought you knew?"

She closed her eyes. Then she opened them, hoping she'd wake up from a fever or something and this would all be a dream. But no, Mach was still there, and the server popped by with their drinks.

"This isn't real," she confirmed. "Not a real date?"

"Not an actual maybe-we-can-make-this-permanent-someday date, if that's what you mean."

"Clearly, I am an idiot." She pressed her fingers to her forehead. All the signs were there, and she hadn't even noticed. Her face flamed; bitterness tasted like a lemon peel settling on her tongue. The bitter taste of believing that something real could come from online dating.

"I'm sorry," he said, and he sounded genuine. But she should be the one to apologize. She was the one who talked down about his band.

"I'm sorry you didn't know it's me you're meeting," he continued.

"Dimefront music is so successful because it's so good," she said quickly. "Ignore everything I said before this statement, yes?" She guzzled club soda through the straw. Set the glass down and then had to hold in a burp because… fizz and guzzling? Didn't go well together.

Awkwardness rolled over them like a thick fog. She shook her head and reached for the club soda again. But, bad idea. Learned that lesson already. The server was right, she'd need something stronger with less carbonation to make all this go away.

"I think I'm gonna go." She snatched her scarf and her purse and started to slide from the—

"Hold up," he winced. "Please don't leave now."

She frowned and then pulled her lips to the side. "Why not?"

"C'mon, it'll look bad, and you didn't even get to meet the band." He ran his tongue over his bottom lip. "I think Bax and Linx will be super interested to hear about your take on our music."

He was clearly joking with that statement, not being mean or anything.

"Um…" What did a person say in this situation? Was there a manual she should consult?

"You have a set soon, then?" she asked, ending her question on a sigh of surrender.

"Yeah." He nodded, keeping his eyes on hers and being

way too chill about her embarrassment. Hard to be upset with a guy when he was being so nice.

"You've got a seat right up front with the other girls," he continued.

"Other girls?" Was he on multiple dates tonight? That's about the only scenario that would make the whole night more cringeworthy. "There are more like me. More dates but not dates?"

He grinned like they were actually having a great time. He was so convincing he almost fooled her, too.

Then he lifted his chin toward the stage. "The other Dimefront guys have their ladies coming and, fair warning, they're all about this thing happening tonight"—he gestured between them—"so be prepared for that."

Wait. Hold the freaking phone.

"Isn't one of the guys with Irina Carmichael?" she asked, squirming a bit, and then setting her stuff back on the bench because she would totally stay to meet Irina.

He nodded. "She's great. You'll love her."

Her mouth dropped open, and she could not get it to close.

This was like one of those waking dreams where a person knew they were dreaming and still wasn't certain if it was going to be a nightmare or a really great story.

"Don't worry. The seating's all set with them. You don't have to do a thing." He smiled like this was a good thing.

"Irina Carmichael is *famous*," Darla pointed out, actually pressing her fingertip to the resin-covered table.

Amusement now danced in his eyes. "She is."

"I'm actually gonna meet her? In person?" She didn't mean to sound so excited, but she definitely couldn't hold it back.

If the date wasn't real, at least this part would make a really great story. She *loved* Irina Carmichael.

"Uh-huh." He toyed with the wrapper from his beer bottle.

"She's amazing. I am a huge fan." Darla may not be on a date with a future partner, but this was pretty amazing.

"You know, some might say that I'm kind of a big deal, too," he said.

"Yeah, totally." She gave him a nod and took a sip of club soda. "You so are." She toyed with the straw and then said, "I'll stick around until the set is done."

She would do this. She would even have fun. There was no risk on this date anymore. It wasn't going anywhere. So she could let this rockstar buy her a drink, play some songs, and then she could move on with her life. Bonus, she'd meet a movie star.

Life was full of other opportunities. This one didn't have to suck.

But another glance at her rockstar for the night—the way his eyes danced and just… the whole package. Her heart tried to pitter-patter more quickly.

She forced it to settle down. No pitter-pattering or flitter-fluttering allowed with this one. Ever.

Chapter Two
MACH

DARLA'S pink lips wrapped around the plastic straw in her drink and damn, but his body took notice. He could not pull his gaze away as she took a long pull of her club soda, then another.

What the hell was wrong with him? He shifted in his seat.

Mach could be an ass. He admitted it. He made snap decisions and stuck with them even if they were disastrous —usually, though, things turned out just fine. Sometimes they didn't.

Like this night with Darla.

Honest to hell, he thought she understood the game. That she didn't? That she came here expecting to meet some dick-face named Mach and maybe try to make a life with him? At least go out a few times? Well, that sat heavy on his chest.

His one redeeming quality? He did like to think he was a *reasonable* ass.

After all, he wanted everyone around him to be comfortable, including Darla. Mach adapted to all situations. He was an excellent chameleon like that. This was an effective tool cultivated early on in his life and sharpened when he joined up with Dimefront.

He'd whip it out for Darla tonight, make sure she had a good time.

And the best way to get a person comfortable so they'd enjoy the moment was to get them to talk about themselves.

"So you've got some strong opinions on music. I like it," he said. Because he did. The whole point of music was how subjective it could be. One person loved jazz, another dug Taylor Swift. There wasn't a rule that everyone had to adore Dimefront.

"Do you play?" he asked.

She flinched. "Yes. A little. When I was a kid."

"Do you shred the guitar?" Then they could have a duet. That could be fun.

She shook her head. "No. No guitar."

"Piano?"

She shook her head again. "Nuh-uh."

"You gonna tell me?"

"Some things are better left in the past." She seemed caught up in a good memory with the way her expression went distant and her lips twisted into a semi-smile.

"Well, now I really want to know."

"I kind of like the guessing game." She folded her hands under her chin.

Then she caught Pam as she passed by. "Do you do frozen cocktails like a piña colada or something? I think I want something stronger."

"Now we're talking," Pam said, under her breath. "We don't, actually. But I have been instructed that you can have whatever you want. So if you want a piña colada? I will have someone run and get a blender. We'll make it happen."

Darla nodded. She caught his gaze.

He nodded back. "That's the rules. You get what you want tonight. Might as well make it good."

Darla bit at her bottom lip. "Do you know that donut shop off of the 16th Street Mall?"

Pam nodded. "I know the one."

Everyone knew that place. Best donuts in Denver.

"They're closed." Darla caught Mach's eyes again, hers sparkling. She was cute when she was having fun. "But I'd really like one of their cream-filled glazed with chocolate and Captain Crunch on top."

Mach sat back and admired her enthusiasm. Not gonna lie, he was a little proud because Darla was going to use her temporary power of "anything you want" not to wreak havoc, or go rent a helicopter, but to get herself the best damn donut around. This was a woman with priorities he could be on board with.

"I'll take one, too," he said.

Pam was all about this. She gave Darla a sly grin. "Let me get that going for you."

Darla's face lit up with excitement. "This is a fun game."

He shifted in his seat, leaning into the table so he didn't have to talk so loud over the crowd. "Why order the club soda before if you really want a fru-fru cocktail?"

"Because before I thought you were legit," she said. "Like a legit date, I mean."

"And I'm not legit?"

"Not now. Being on my best behavior mattered then. Now? Not so much. I'm free to ask for donuts and piña coladas." She rubbed her hands together like an evil genius cartoon.

"What's it like being a nurse?" he asked. That was a safe question and it showed that he did care about her life outside of this bar. "Takes a special kind of person to do what you do."

She took a small sip from her glass and fiddled with the straw. "It's like you are helping people and some really appreciate what you do. But then not everyone wants to be helped. And then you get puked on. Very glamorous."

"Pretty sweet that you save lives for a living," he said instead of asking her to do the straw thing again with her mouth so he could watch.

Instead, he listened as she told him all about how she preferred to give an IV in the forearm because the patient has more mobility, even if it's harder for her as the nurse. About how her favorite pen to chart with had the super fine tip but was really hard to find, and how she hated the word Flumazenil because it tasted weird when she said it.

"Sorry. That's enough about me," she said, abruptly cutting herself off. "I mean, you make people happy with music for a living. That's pretty fantastic."

Mach nodded.

"I never know how the music might affect someone. And when it does, it's a powerful thing. But, uh, why'd you stop telling me about your job?" Mach asked, catching her gaze with his and holding it there.

"You're being very nice to me and that's really nice of you." Darla held her hands together in her lap. "But there's no way you really want to hear all of the mundane details about my job."

"Who's saying what I really want to hear about?" he asked, settling deeper into the bench seat. "This is interesting."

"Even I know that it's not." She brushed her hair off of her shoulder. "I mean this is fun, you know," she said, gesturing to the bar at large. "But the whole not-really-a-date thing is a surprise. And I don't really like surprises. Even the nice ones. I prefer predictable."

"Where's the fun in that?" he asked, polishing off the ginger ale he passed off as beer. A trick he learned from the veteran Dimefront guys. Save the street cred, but don't get sloshed before a show.

"Life isn't always about having fun," Darla said. "It's not all piña coladas."

"Why can't it be?" he asked. What was the point if you didn't at least enjoy the life you got to live?

"I could give you my lecture that I give the patients who arrive in an ambulance after a night of entirely too much fun and zero predictability. I've got a whole spiel ready when we're done with the stomach pump," she said. "But I won't do that to you."

"I don't know, maybe I'd like to hear it." He leaned in closer, elbows on the table.

She met him halfway, so they were sharing space there in the middle.

"There is a rhythm to understanding how things should be," she said. "How they work best. That's how you get to the good stuff. It can't all be fun and games."

He didn't want to catch feelings for her. He didn't. He wouldn't. But he was actually enjoying this conversation.

"What's your story, Darla?" he asked her, but also asked himself.

"Met a guy. Got engaged. You know the rest." She pushed her hair behind her ear.

His eyebrows pulled together. "Don't think I do."

"It didn't work out. Things happen." Was she trying to convince him or her?

"Fiancé did the whole it's-not-you-it's-me song and dance a few months back. Then he tossed me out on my ass. Just like that, my now-and-forever became a total asshat. And when all of that went to hell in a handbasket, I moved in with my friend and licked my wounds. Then I pulled myself together, and now I'm here."

Mach squirmed a little.

She pushed a lock of hair behind her ear. "I'd been with him since undergrad."

He nodded along until that point. Then he shook his head. "Relationships that start when you're a kid never last."

"That's not true." She clearly didn't like that. "And we weren't kids."

"You were in college?" he asked, his interest level increasing as he spoke.

She nodded. "Yes."

"You were kids." He said this like he knew. But he didn't. He didn't know. Not really.

Darla's lips pressed into a thin line.

Shit, he'd said the wrong thing.

Pam came by to let them know a blender had been purchased, the donuts were somehow on the way, thanks to Hans. Hans, whose connections knew no bounds.

Darla ordered another seltzer, but the spark from earlier had dimmed.

"Are you okay?" Mach asked. Which was stupid because she was clearly not okay, and he probably shouldn't be asking her that. "I'm sorry if I hit a nerve." He was.

"No, the crazy thing is that you're right," she said, totally serious. "I mean, where has predictability gotten me?"

"Right here with me?" He didn't mean it as a joke, but rather... hey, you won a contest you didn't even know you entered!

Now she laughed. Started as a chuckle and built into full belly laughs.

He laughed with her, even though he wasn't certain why they were laughing. Not exactly.

But she couldn't seem to stop. She held her side as he continued to laugh.

This could get uncomfortable.

"Did you play the trumpet?" he asked, going back to their game from before.

She shook her head again.

"You're persistent. All right, fine. I played the…" She did a drum roll on the table with her hands. "Clarinet."

Now that he did not expect, but—

"I've always had a soft spot for woodwinds," he teased.

She tossed her hair over her shoulder and his eyes followed the movement. "I'll have you know, I was first chair as a senior in high school."

He let out a low whistle. "Now that is impressive."

Something seemed to shift inside her.

"I know this whole thing is for show," she said, resigned. "It's not like you actually want to be here with me."

A pang of guilt hit him in the chest. "That's not—"

She held up her wait-a-minute hand. "I appreciate the effort you're making here. I do. But you don't have to. Really. I'll hang out so it looks good. You don't have to try, though. You don't want to hear about my failed relationships or the crap I put up with at work. It's sweet of you to ask. But I get it. I'm a prop. It's all good."

Well, fuck. He didn't want her to think he was only using her. Then again, he sort of was, and that wasn't okay.

It was almost time to take the stage with the band, so he showed her the way to the table reserved for the girls up front. Darla moved beside him, and their arms brushed a little as the crowd jostled them and pushed them together. He had to put his arm around her waist, so they didn't get separated. He liked that she let him. Liked how natural her body felt next to his. How she smelled of vanilla and he wanted to live in that scent. In the moment.

The thing is, Mach lived the rockstar dream. But, honestly, sometimes he felt like he was only going through the motions, never really opening himself up to anyone. Not really.

Sure, Dimefront gave him purpose and a steady paycheck, but was it enough? Did he need something more?

He hadn't actually thought that might be true, until these moments. Until Darla let him off the hook. Until he introduced her to the wives and girlfriends, watching from the stage as she settled in with them.

By the time the band hit the third song, a couple of pitchers of piña coladas appeared on their table along with a dozen donuts topped with breakfast cereal.

And Darla barely looked up at the stage the whole time.

That was her choice, he didn't have a say in it at all. But it bugged him. And he couldn't figure out exactly why.

Chapter Three
DARLA

TWO PIÑA COLADAS (and a couple of donuts) in and she was on a serious sugar kick. And a mega rock 'n roll high. Because Mach on stage with his guitar? In those jeans? With those tats? Darla was absolutely salivating.

Yup, she was now and forever officially a Ten—the pet name Dimefront gave to their groupies. Everything she said before about Dimefront being too commercial? She took it all back, because up there, on the stage, the guys weren't playing music. They were the music.

She'd never experienced music like this before. Not that she was a regular at Red Rocks for concerts or anything, but she'd been to a few. Tonight she was captivated by each note, each lyric, and every move Mach made on the stage.

The bass lines reverberated through her body like an electric current, and she swayed with the beat. The energy from the band radiated through the room, palpable enough to touch and tangible enough to make her feel like she was actually in the song. Honestly, the whole experience was like an invitation to join in on the journey. Like being part of something seriously special for a few bars.

Also, she loved the Dimefront ladies.

Irina was so down to earth. Courtney and Becca were extra fun. And Sami Jo was the sweetest. It was like being at work with the other nurses. They all just clicked so easily.

The one thing that made her shift uncomfortably in her seat? Mach's piercing gaze lingering on her from the stage. Looking at her like she was the only one in the room. He didn't need to slather on more of that sex appeal. Sex appeal that she enjoyed, but that would get her absolutely nowhere but heartbreak because then she'd start thinking tonight was more than it was, and it was not going to be *that*.

Back at their table, when he'd asked her all about herself, she let him. Told him about being a nurse, all the little things no one ever cared about. He even asked questions to keep the conversation moving. There she was, chattering away about things of no consequence to *anyone* outside of the hospital, much less someone like Mach. And he'd listened.

They crushed one of their iconic hits, and Bax—the front man—took control of the mic and bellowed, "Y'all know my man Mach is out here at Brek's tonight on some wild rendezvous."

The bar erupted into wild cheers. Bax pointed to Darla and declared. "This is Darla. She's here with Mach. They met on what… Nocturnal Cupid?"

The wild cheers whipped into a frenzy. And Darla? Right there in the center of it all, thanks to a bit of rum and a hefty helping of sugar. She waved her arms around and blew kisses like it was nothing—something she would never do. Not without the liquid courage and the Captain Crunch.

"Let's get to know each other like fam, what do ya

say?" Bax asked, sitting on the edge of the stage with a playful confidence as if this were a real question and answer session.

Darla nodded because… rum.

"Let's do it," she shouted, snatching her drink and heading to the stage.

The other Dimefront ladies went absolutely wild at her agreement. The venue shook with shouts and applause as Bax gestured for Mach to join him on the edge of the stage. Mach set his guitar aside and moseyed that way. His gaze? It never left Darla.

Bax made room for Darla to join him. And she hopped right up on the stage like she had every right to be there.

"So, Darla… you won a contest, huh? How's it going so far tonight?" Bax asked like he was Dr. Phil.

Mach's gaze seized hers and she was putty. Pure putty.

"It's going good," she said. "But, uh, you know, I came tonight because I thought this was an actual date." She paused, chewed on that for a moment. Then asked the audience, "Can you even believe that?"

Bax laughed. The audience laughed. Mach's expression turned impassive.

"To be honest, I'm glad this isn't real," she continued. "I mean, can you even imagine? Me with *him*?" The snort laugh came out all on its own.

Oh God, that had happened. Her cheeks heated. She held her hand over her mouth.

But Bax was on it, draping his arm over her shoulder. Mic in his other hand, he turned to Mach with what seemed to be practiced ease. "You got anything to add?"

Mach was frowning. Likely because she'd just snorted in front of everyone. Tomorrow she'd hate that she did that. Tonight, she smiled to encourage him along.

He took the mic. He looked at her like he was the one who won the dating game.

"What's wrong with you and me?" he finally asked.

That got the audience all kinds of riled up—including the Dimefront ladies.

"Mach," she pulled the mic to her mouth and said his name, gently. "You and I are from totally different worlds. There's no reason to mix things that don't belong together. I don't do celebrities. They don't do me. It's like our little thing."

She said this with a whole lotta sass and a hefty helping of confidence.

"Bullshit," he said under his breath. Then he added, "Have you ever had a shot with someone famous?"

"No. Of course not." Also, hold up. She looked to the audience. "Did he just bullshit me?"

Bax was totally loving this. The audience ate it up. And Darla? Darla was on it—just letting herself enjoy the moment.

Mach's jaw went slack at her declaration and the dare in his eyes was clear as the sun setting on the Rockies.

"Wait," she continued. "Let's be honest with ourselves. No one here believes we could be more than two people on a publicity date."

"Not with that attitude, they won't," he countered.

Bax moved the mic back and forth with an ease that seemed practiced.

"You don't like predictability," she announced. "And it's practically listed on my name tag at work."

The way Mach stared at her made her squirm in an uncomfortable new way. Uncomfortable and something else… excited?

"How do you know what I like or don't like?" he asked, and then the audience and Bax and the Dimefront ladies, they all slipped into the background. This was only the two of them having a conversation.

"Mach." She lifted her eyebrows. "You are a rockstar. It's not hard to put it together."

Now that? That brought on a smile from him. He full-on beamed like it was a good thing.

"Nothing about…well…you…says anything but roll with it," she continued, since she was marching on toward whatever point this was becoming.

"And you don't roll with it?" he asked, as though he had paid zero attention to anything she'd said up to that point.

She shook her head anyway in answer to his question.

"You know what my life needs right now?" she asked.

"Bet you're gonna tell me." That damn dimple high on his cheek above the beard made an appearance.

Honestly, it was a good thing this whole shebang was a farce. Because, if this date *were* real, there was a chance she would've seriously enjoyed his attention. It would totally toss her off kilter. Have her questioning things that didn't need questioning.

"Better predictability," she said. "That's what my life needs right now." More stability. Maybe she should go for something totally predictable like that Nurses on the Frontline program she'd been thinking about. Her entire day would be mapped out for her. All she would have to do is show up.

She gulped at what seemed like an a-ha moment.

"I have an idea." Mach said this low, like it was only for her. The words were sultry. Gravelly. Yummy.

And then it wasn't only them. The rest of the room came into focus. Bax between them. The mic at Mach's lips as he said, "Spend tonight with me."

The room zipped to a pinprick. *Did he just…? Had he just…?*

Spend tonight with me. That's what he'd said. Like he was fresh off the set of a daytime soap opera show. Yes, he'd said it! To her, no less. In front of *everybody*.

Frozen in space, she did nothing but take a decent pull of her piña colada. Not the best choice, because when a piece of coconut got caught against her throat, she had to choke it down. She did her best to do it without too much fanfare.

He paused before saying anything else. Appearing to ensure she wouldn't stop breathing before he said anything else.

Mach waited, and dammit, he was so gorgeous. He was so far out of her league that he played a different sport. But here he was, watching her lips like she'd dribbled piña colada on them, and he seriously wanted to lick it off.

She shivered.

No. No shivering. No flutters. She had to respond first.

He hadn't said something simple like, "Let's hang out." Nor had he asked something direct like, "Wanna fuck?" This was a situation that required a whole heaping spoonful of clarity.

"Are you asking me to hook up?" she asked.

The smolder in his gaze was enough to warm even the coldest blended cocktail.

"Let me show you how fun things get when you let them be," he said instead of a direct answer. And the husky tone of his words made her whole body hum. There was a crackle in the air between them. Some kind of chemical induced promise happening.

No one—not even Tom—had ever made that happen before. Tom hadn't ever spoken to her with anything but a perfunctory effort that did not elicit whole-body hums.

Mach stared at her like he saw things even she didn't know yet. Her mouth went dry.

The only logical conclusion was that she was misunderstanding. She shook her head, trying to make the moths stop flitting around in her brain so she could think.

Nooo, he was *not* asking her to hook up. Even if that was precisely what it sounded like. This was not some kind of hot-guy pickup line and a way to save face in front of all these people. Although, given that she was a noob to this entire experience, she wasn't totally certain.

So she took another sip of her drink.

Swallowed it thoroughly this time.

Got it down with zero issues.

Then she wiped her mouth with her fingertip, since she was going to need to keep her wits in place and come from a sound position of power. A girl couldn't do that with the prospect of dribble on her chin.

"Or," she said, ready to offer the only acceptable alternative to whatever it was he was suggesting. "I'm going to finish this phenomenal cocktail." She pointed to the drink. "Then I'm going to eat an entire donut—with no help." That last part seemed like an important bit to add. "And then we'll go our separate ways." Yes, perfect amount of strength in that statement. *Well done, Darla!* "Maybe we'll see each other again on some dating site? Who knows?" She lifted a shoulder, then focused on her drink.

He said nothing, and it's not like she could look up at him. If she did that, then she'd have to acknowledge that she'd just turned him down without even being certain he'd asked her to do anything beyond a game of Yahtzee. So, no, she didn't look up. But even without looking, she knew he hadn't moved.

If she wasn't who she was, then of course she'd say yes to his offer. He was attractive, with all that sex appeal oozing all over the stage. There was no doubt why women fell under his spell and came out as a notch on his belt buckle.

The taste of pineapple soured at the thought, and she firmed every ounce of resolve because she wasn't a notch. Not a notch kind of girl.

She was the girl that guys married. The kind they brought home to their family.

Fine. That she'd never been married? Not her fault. Tom's family had adored her, though. One out of two wasn't bad.

"You are thinking awful hard for a woman who just shot him down," Bax said, studying her and then Mach.

Mach was clearly not perturbed in the slightest. His eyes danced with humor, but no mischief. Like he enjoyed her being off kilter. Not that he was relieved or anything.

"That's really what you want to do?" he questioned, and the way he asked seemed more than genuine. "Stick with the predictable?"

No. But, also, "Yes."

She didn't even slightly choke on the word because Mach was the king of the bad boys, and she couldn't allow that into her life.

"Your call," Mach said. Something switching off in his expression.

And that was that. The band started up with another song, Mach and Bax eased her off the stage with their banter and laughter. Then they jumped right in like the little public conversation wasn't a big thing at all.

And when the band was done with their set, and the Dimefront ladies all paired off with their guys and headed off, she and Mach were by themselves in a little back room by the kitchen.

"Thank you for a really fun night." Darla wasn't sure at

all what to do with her hands, so she just let them rest at her sides.

"I meant what I said up there." The intensity of who he was seemed to wrap around her and hang on. "Let's ditch the predictability and have a little fun."

She nibbled at her bottom lip, because part of her wanted to say yes. But that part was only a sliver and the rest of her was way more logical.

"Let's, uh, pretend for a moment that you are enjoying yourself with me and actually want to be here."

"I'm on board." The extra twinkle in his eye was unnecessary.

"Here's what will happen if I keep talking." This wasn't hard to see coming.

"I'm dying to hear. I love when someone knows the future. Makes it easier for me," Mach said.

"You'll ask me lots of questions. I'll have fun talking about all the things no one ever asks me about. I'll loosen up and move to rum shots. Then I'll be horribly embarrassed. I'll go home to the bedroom I'm renting from my friend. You'll go to your penthouse downtown. I'll realize how ridiculous I sounded. You'll realize these are seconds you'll never get back." She fluttered her eyelashes. Was it dramatic? Uh-huh. Would she do it again? Also, uh-huh.

"I don't live in a penthouse downtown," he said, deadpan.

"Belcaro then?" she asked. Her best friend, Patrice, had dated a man who grew up in that neighborhood. Talk about posh. The garages practically came with their own garages.

He shook his head. "Nope."

Huh. He lived in Denver. Everyone knew the Dime-front guys lived here. Which only left—

"I didn't peg you as a golfer with a country club

house." Though she didn't know him. Not really. For all she knew, he played with a foursome every Saturday.

"Cherry Hills Village," he said, under his breath, before lifting a bottle of water to his lips.

His lips. That bottle. The way his throat worked as he swallowed. He went all in, just like he probably did in the bedroom.

Her stomach did the flippy thing again.

But he'd said something. What was it he'd said?

"Sorry, what?" She didn't mean to blush, she'd just had a significantly dirty thought about him—

"Cherry Hills Village. That's where I live." He quirked his head to the side. "You can stop guessing now that you know." He kicked off from the wall, moving toward her. "Now it's my turn to tell the future."

"I can't wait to hear it," she said with way more confidence than she actually felt.

"We're going to go our separate ways," he said.

Wasn't that pretty much what she'd said?

"But." He leaned in an inch closer. "Next time I'm in the hospital, I'm going to ask for that forearm IV because now I know. And you? Well, eventually, you're going to realize that you could actually do something fun for yourself, and when that happens, you're going to call me."

Hello, Mr. Presumptuous.

"That will not happen," she assured.

"Why not?"

She returned his sly smile from earlier and played her winning hand. "I just won't take your number."

Chapter Four
MACH

HONEST AS ALL HELL, Mach tried to erase Darla Davis from his brain. Yet it seemed like she was welded into his memory as one of those persistent flashbacks that wouldn't leave him alone. Which meant he was screwed.

What did a guy do when he was screwed? He floated on a pizza slice in his pool. An inflatable slice. Let the sun beat down on his face and tried to burn away all thoughts from the other night. Then he hoped like hell he'd find the drive to get off the pizza, and get on with his life.

"He's going to melt into that pool toy," Hans said.

Mach didn't open his eyes to see who Hans spoke to because it didn't matter. Not really. They'd all ride his ass about getting out of the pool and on with his life. The usual suspects would be any of his bandmates or their women: Linx and Becca, Bax and Courtney, Knox and Irina, or Tanner and Samantha.

"We all have our own coping mechanisms," Becca said. "He's not hurting anyone. As long as he's wearing sunscreen. You wearing sunscreen, Mach?"

He grunted and gave a thumbs up. He took back what

he thought before. This is why he liked Becca. She kept her nose out of his shit.

"Let him handle his rejection in this somewhat healthy manner," Becca continued.

Nope, didn't like the rejection word since that's not what had happened. But Becca was a licensed professional counselor, so she knew all kinds of stuff and he would let it slide. Still, the word stung.

"Mach, these kinds of emotions are all new to you. Float away your uncertainty," Becca continued.

Yeah, he'd always liked Becca. She was the bomb.

"At least for now," she continued. "Soon you'll have to actually deal with it."

He scowled and took back his original train of thought: she was as bad as the rest of them.

"Stop kicking yourself about the date," Tanner said with a splash.

Mach peeled open his eyes to find his best friend climbing atop an inflatable, adult-size Taco Bell Hot Sauce packet. The getting situated part wasn't going so well, but Tanner didn't have as much practice as Mach in this area, so that was to be expected.

"Give him a break, he's not used to rejection," Sam said. "It hurts."

There was that rejection word again.

Sam had settled in on one of the lounge chairs on the pool deck. Since she and Tanner coupled up, she had practically moved in. Mach figured it wouldn't be long before they made it official with rings, a wedding, and kids. The house where they lived was fucking huge, so Mach didn't mind another roommate.

Sam was good for Tanner. And she loved him, so even if Mach had had issues with the situation—and he didn't —he wouldn't have said a peep.

"How long until he's better?" Hans asked in that matter-of-fact way of his.

"Healing happens in its own time," Becca replied. "Public rejection from a woman he's interested in is hard. Especially when he's not used to it."

Mach squeezed open an eye, squinting against the bright sun. That's the third time they'd used that word in only minutes.

"I did not get rejected," he assured.

"Okay," Becca said, but the way she said it sounded like she was only giving lip service.

"How long until he admits he got rejected?" Sam asked.

Hans snort laughed at that. Sounded more like he choked, but whatever.

"Stop saying that word," Mach said, losing the joy of the float. "We ended the date on fine terms." He dropped his hand over the side of the pizza into the cool water with enough force to make a splash.

"It was fine?" Hans asked. "Which is why you've been pouting ever since?"

"It's not his fault." Tanner was the one Mach could count on. "He's not used to pretty girls telling him no."

Apparently, Mach couldn't count on him this time.

He growled. "Can't a dude catch a break without everyone reminding him of his screw ups?"

"Not around here," Tanner said, finally done with his water acrobatics and settled on his sauce packet, floating to the other side of the pool.

"Hey, Mach?" Sam asked.

He harrumphed in reply.

"I think everyone is actually worried about you," she said, serious in a way that made him pause. "We all joke, but you're not yourself since…well…you know."

An uncomfortable blanket of silence fell over the pool area.

Hans cleared his throat as though trying to clear the awkwardness single-handedly.

"Why doesn't everyone go inside, and we can all stick our noses into Sam's business instead?" Becca suggested.

"That sounds fun," Sam replied. "I'm in."

There was a scraping of the metal chair against the concrete as the loungers were rearranged, back to their usual positions.

"You two are on your own," Hans said, gruff as usual. "We're gonna go eat some cheese sticks and talk about Sam."

Ever since Sam had been exposed as Sami Jo—the pop sensation—Hans had begun working with her to get her settled in the industry. Mach enjoyed having her around. Enjoyed having them all around. But he appreciated the quiet as everyone but Tanner headed back to the house.

Tanner would know that Mach didn't want to talk it out. He'd understand the value of quiet. The only sound being that of the pool lapping against the stairs.

"So..." Tanner said, the little splashes of his hands in the water a telltale sign he was paddling closer. "What's new?"

On second thought, perhaps, Mach had given him too much credit on the understanding part.

"Can we not?" Mach asked, folding his hands across his chest, and letting the Vitamin D from the sun do its thing and infuse him with a hit of happiness. "I want to lie here and think about nothing."

"Okay," Tanner agreed, chipper as fuck. "We'll float here while you don't think about Darla."

Mach snort laughed at that announcement.

The date *had* ended on fine terms. Darla even took the

time to do a few quick pics for the photographers out front of the bar. He walked her to her purple VW Bug. What had he expected her to drive? He didn't know, but her vehicle was so Darla he couldn't help but dig it.

That had been that.

She drove away and still—

"It's like she's there. In my brain like a bongo solo that won't stop," Mach said. "I can't get her to stop."

"I know the feeling," Tanner replied.

He and Sam were still fairly new. And they'd had some challenges. But their situation was different because they were perfect for each other. That much was clear from the beginning.

"Darla doesn't even like me," Mach said to Tanner. To himself. To the world at large.

The last time he'd been rejected so thoroughly was during his first high school experience. Before he knew the importance of checking vulnerability at the door. Before everything got fucked. Before he'd gone to live with Dan, and met Tanner, dropped out for good and finished up with a GED instead of a diploma. Dan was the foster dad who took him in. Tanner was the foster brother who gave him purpose. They were his found family, and they'd introduced him to Dimefront. His forever family.

He didn't know much about his parents, and he didn't understand a lot about family. They'd died when he was still too little to remember, and there wasn't any extended family to take him in. Friends did for a while, but he was a hard kid going through some serious stuff. He was... unlovable.

"She saves lives," Mach said, rubbing his hands over his face.

He was a rock star by accident. How it all went down? No one would believe him. If he hadn't lived it, he wouldn't either. But Dimefront wasn't only a band to Mach, they were his family.

So he was a rock star by accident, but Darla saved lives on the regular on purpose.

When Tanner said nothing else, Mach kept going. "I mean, she was seriously not into me."

"That sounds like a stretch. I saw the way she looked at you."

Mach lifted a shoulder. The shit of this whole thing was that he wasn't interested in anything long term, anyway. Didn't do long term. Hell, he didn't do relationships. He hooked up. Kept things light.

But when Darla told him no? Well, the flicker of uncertainty bloomed in his chest in a way he hadn't felt in ages. That was a place he hadn't been in a long fucking time.

"It's okay to like her," Tanner said, gentle like this was the territory that would get him knocked off his sauce packet. "I mean, if she's got the power to get in your head, she must be pretty special."

They were quiet for a bit, letting the pool work its magic.

"You know, when you put yourself on Nocturnal Cupid, I actually thought it was a good idea," Tanner said. This was a surprise because everyone rode Mach's ass about it.

Mach cracked an eyelid and lifted his sunglasses to get a better look at Tanner. "Why the hell would you think that?"

"Because it is a good idea for you to go out on a date. Get to know an actual person. Not just…"

Not a secret that Mach hooked up. It's what he did. It was safe. No attachment and no feelings. But Tanner had found his slice of happy and apparently he wanted Mach to get a taste of the same.

"Keep your heart eyes out of my life," Mach said with a laugh and a decent splash of pool water. He rolled off the pizza slice into the cold. It enveloped him, holding his body in stasis to float between where he came from and where he was headed. But he couldn't stay that way forever. So he swam to the surface, then to the side. He couldn't say for certain where he was headed next. Probably off to fuck up the next thing.

"Mach, time to get out of the pool," Hans said, marching toward the pool with Becca on his heels. Sam wasn't far behind them.

Mach nodded, shaking the droplets from his hair. "Yeah, I know. I'm off the damn slice."

Moving on with life.

"A dating-advice influencer posted about your date," Becca said, hurrying behind Hans, and out of breath.

"Yeah?" he asked. "That's good for the band."

Maybe something decent would come from all of this. More than the initial deflection of attention off of Tanner.

"They dissected the conversation you had on stage with Darla and Bax." Becca grimaced.

"With emphasis on the part where Darla turned you down," Hans said.

"It's a… thing," Becca added.

That the date was getting the band some attention? Excellent news.

That the part that was picked up was his humiliation? Not so much.

That pizza slice looked pretty damn good right about then. It practically called to him, inviting him to climb on up.

"Define *thing*," Mach said, already knowing he wasn't going to like the answer.

"Darla is now very popular," Hans said.

That would be good if Darla wanted the popularity. But Darla didn't seem like she'd be down with any of this. She'd only wanted to go on a date and meet someone. Not be the center of attention for some influencer's attempt at likes and clicks.

"And I'm…?" Mach asked.

"Your image is taking a hit." Hans had no emotion as he gave the news. The guy could be telling Mach he wanted oat milk for his cereal or that Mach's public image was being shredded. It came out the same either way.

Mach didn't love that his image was gonna need some TLC, but he'd deal with it.

Unfortunately, Mach wasn't new to this type of attention from the tabloids. His throat went tight because—Darla? Darla was.

"Is this gonna fuck with her life?" Mach finally asked, even though he already knew the answer.

No one answered, so Mach answered for himself. "It's gonna fuck with her life."

"You know how you always said you didn't mind being branded as the Dimefront asshole?" Becca asked.

Mach nodded. Of all the shit to care about, that never seemed like something to get worked up about.

"Congrats, it happened," Hans concluded.

"Darla's the opposite. Everyone's hoping she'll find Mr. Perfect out of all this," Becca said as she made a hand motion that probably wasn't supposed to be lewd, but it was.

"Is anyone even putting us together?" Mach asked. "Hoping *we'll* be a couple?"

"No," Hans said without even a hint of apology. He cleared his throat.

Mach tried to ignore how that word settled heavy in

the back of his throat because he didn't want a relation-ship. He didn't.

Since it was summer, everything was warm. But right then, the heat got worse. Mach didn't like the way the sun pounded on his skin from one side and his blood from the other. Everything seemed tight. He tried to shake it off, but it didn't work. So he pulled himself up to the pool deck and out of the water. Droplets of water slid over his face, down his arms. He reached for the oversized, white towel he'd set out earlier.

"We need to get ahold of Darla," he said, toweling off his abdomen and arms. "Make sure she's got whatever she needs, so this *doesn't* screw with her life."

Any more than it already had.

"Your girl's not answering her phone," Hans said. "Called the emergency room, but they're not saying shit about if she's working or not. I'm about to head to the hospital. See if I can track her down."

Hold up. "You got her number?"

"Follow along, kid." Hans said this like he was talking to a toddler. "Of course I collected her information. But it doesn't matter because I can't reach her."

Tension pulled between Mach's shoulder blades. He didn't like any of this. Not one bit.

Chapter Five
DARLA

DARLA ADORED all that she accomplished in her job. But even someone who loves the purpose of what they do can get bored with the monotony of day to day. There was, however, one good part of working at the same hospital as her best friends. They might be in the middle of another same ol', same ol' shift, but they had each other. Renata worked in the recovery room, and Patrice was a nurse in labor and delivery.

Darla had dished all about her date with Mach. Renata and Patrice wanted more details so they could, as a group, evaluate everything that happened.

"I'm not talking about it anymore," Darla said, eyeing her friends in the staff lounge of their hospital. The canary-yellow walls needed a fresh coat of paint, but that wasn't happening soon. The staff areas weren't the most important for aesthetics. The big bosses saved those dollars for patient areas. That's why the dings in the drywall and permanent scuffs along the bottom rubber wall base wouldn't be going anywhere for a long time.

"Who should I use for a referral endorsement?" She

chewed at her lip as she flipped through the ledger in her head of all of those who would say nice things about her. She needed a big name for this. Somebody with a spotless reputation and at least a few papers published in the past two years.

"Can we please put a pin in your Frontline application?" Patrice asked, flipping the page on her embossed white wedding planner. "For now."

Patrice had picked an accountant as her fixer-upper, not a doctor. It turned out that was a good choice.

Now, Patrice was well on her way to wedded bliss, and Darla was… not. While Patrice planned her wedding, Darla stared at the Frontline application she'd opened on her laptop.

Clearly, online dating was not going to work for her. So she thought about what would make her happier, and, honestly? It wasn't a man in her life.

She'd always thought traveling overseas with an organization like Frontline might be a kick. A predictable, controlled-environment kick. The idea appealed to the part of herself that wanted to make things better for others. Even the part of her that needed to heal. Maybe it wouldn't be fun all the time, but it would be new, and it would be interesting, and there would probably be some good times mixed in. Plus, they would expect her to fix stuff. That was the entire purpose of the organization.

While Mach might think that fun for her should be a rockstar night out, she knew herself better than that.

So, she seriously looked into the program. Then it was natural that she started the application process.

"If there's one thing that Mach showed me," Darla said, "it's that I am ready to move on with my life. It's time. And the more I think about it, it is time for a big change. I mean, why not? Mom and Dad are in South Dakota."

They'd moved to be near her brother, his wife, and his new baby. "Tom and I are done." It didn't sting to say it that time. "And I can't live in your guest room forever." That left… Nurses on the Frontline.

"No Frontline." Renata shook her head. "It'll take you away from us."

Unfortunately, Patrice and Renata hated the idea of Darla applying for a Frontline position because then she could get accepted. And if she got accepted, she would take it. There was some prestige there. They accepted less than eight percent of applicants. Before she'd fussed about applying because she worried about running water, but now the icky feelings came when she realized how many nurses sought this opportunity. Which meant, if she got that acceptance, she'd be leaving for a year or more.

Her friends did not like that.

"Think about it," Renata said, folding her hands under her chin. "You don't really want to move away. I don't want you to move away. So you shouldn't move away."

"Excellent points," Patrice added, forking a bit of cafeteria meatloaf.

"Who's moving away?" Mario—the pediatrics intern—asked. He pulled up a chair, turned it around, and straddled it before folding his arms over the back.

"Darla." Renata scowled as she said this. "She's filling out a Frontline application."

"Is this because Dr. Damaged screwed you over?" Mario asked, absolutely oblivious to the fact that Tom should stay out of lunchtime conversation.

"What would make you stay?" Patrice asked, clearly ready to go out and get that thing.

Finding a reason to stay…

A person worth staying for…

She didn't say any of that out loud. They all knew it anyway.

"Here's what I'm going to do," she said, pressing her palms into the table to assist as she scooted back her chair.

"I hope she says, 'log into my Nocturnal Cupid account,'" Renata said with a sigh because she knew Darla well enough to know that was not where Darla was going with this.

"I'm going back to work. I'm going to do my very best to save a few lives. And then I'm going to ask Dr. Anthony for a Frontline reference." This put a little skip in her step. As long as she focused on how great this would be, she wouldn't start drifting into what-ifs about running water or where she'd buy toiletries. And she definitely would not have her mind wandering toward Mach.

She saved the application, closed her laptop, tossed her trash into the receptacle, and—

"Hey, Darla?" Patrice asked, flipping through her phone.

Darla didn't even blink before she said, "If you are swiping right for me on any more dates, I'm going to lose—"

"Darla." Patrice looked up, her expression totally unreadable.

Patrice never looked concerned or pained. This was the mask she slid into place instead. The one only her good friends could decipher. The look that got Darla to stop in her tracks and made gravity feel stronger.

"Have you checked your messages?" Patrice asked, the question squeaking a touch at the end.

"No. I haven't looked. Why?" Darla asked

"Oh hell," Mario said, glancing at his phone, too. His eyebrows drew together. "Darla…"

Darla glanced at Renata, who looked like she sucked on lemons for lunch.

Whatever it was, it was something. She scooted back to Patrice and glanced at the screen.

A grainy video played as a reel on repeat. A grainy video of Darla on her date with Mach. There was commentary. Loads of commentary.

Her stomach sank.

"It seems the publicity from your publicity stunt seems to have gotten a lot of publicity," Mario said, eyes wide.

Yep, gravity was definitely working overtime. The nerve endings in her fingertips weren't though, they'd gone off duty seeing how her fingers lost all feeling.

This was at the point when Mach had asked her to spend the night with him. The subtitles made that much clear. Also, it was only two days ago, so she remembered.

"Oh." Darla braced her hand against the back of Patrice's chair. She tried for a no-big-deal exterior, but inside she was a crumbling hot mess.

"There's more." Mario held up his screen so she could watch as she checked off how the evening would go with Mach while predicting the future on their date.

"How did this even happen?" Numb fingers notwithstanding, she reached for Mario's cell. There were so many comments. Like, a lot of comments. Cold reality was setting in past her fingers all throughout her body.

No, she wouldn't look at the comments. She could set a boundary there.

Shit. She was one hundred percent going to look.

As the video ran on a loop, she pressed the comments icon, but before she could read anything, Mario snatched his phone back. He shook his head. "That's a bad idea."

"Maybe don't read the comments." Renata pursed her

lips. "Nothing good ever comes from the comments section."

"Except you are very popular for standing your ground," Patrice added, apparently reading the comments. "*Very* popular."

Darla caught herself clenching her front teeth together. She stopped. Took a deep inhale.

"This is going to be a big deal, isn't it?" Darla asked, resigned because this was obvious, of course. But saying it out loud seemed to make it more real. When it became real, she could work on accepting it.

Patrice nodded. "Apparently."

Then it was with rubber legs that Darla stood and reassured everyone, saying, "This is okay. I've always wanted to be popular. Always wondered what it'd be like. Yeah, this is okay."

Perhaps if she said that enough, it would be true.

Chapter Six
DARLA

THIS WAS NOT OKAY.

"This cannot be happening." Darla pressed her fingertips against her temples.

But hell, it *was* happening. Really happening. Her breaths came way too quick sitting in the hospital's Human Resources naughty chair. Because in this upside-down version of the world, influencers kept trying to sneak into the ER to snap a picture of Darla. Don't even get her started on the overflow of men wanting to proposition her —finding reasons to be admitted in the hope she'd be the nurse assigned. Reasons that were clogging up the whole triage system.

Darla was the talk of Datestagram—the dating section of Instagram. Which made her the talk of the hospital. Which made her the talk of Denver.

From there, things spiraled. All since lunch.

"Even if we weren't rerouting ambulances because of the immense attention in the Emergency Department, and increasing security because everyone wants to talk to you, the fact is you're so recognizable right now we can't put you back on the floor. You're a distraction to the other staff, and the patients. We absolutely can't have anyone else risking tetanus because they want to date you," Trixie, the Human Resources lead, said. She grimaced as she said "tetanus."

Darla did, too, because the guy who pretended to impale his finger with a rusty nail so Darla would be his nurse took things entirely too far.

Trixie's eyes softened as she said, "This solution is only until things blow over. We have to think about the patients first."

Darla understood. "I get it. I do."

When she'd gone back to work after lunch, the nonsense had already begun. It started with one Instagram influencer checking herself in, but she quickly was identified and got shuffled outside. By the fourth check-in, Darla realized it wasn't a one-off and this was going to be an issue because all the non-emergencies showing up definitely put a cramp in patient care.

The hospital's public relations department even had to get involved.

And now she was officially instructed to take a leave of absence. A paid leave of absence, but she wouldn't get all the overtime that fed her Frappuccino addiction and her love of new shoes.

Standing from the chair, she held her head high as she took her walk of shame out the door. And there was Tom, standing in the hallway. Waiting for her. That's the moment Darla fully hated this day. Being popular was definitely not as fun as it sounded.

Tom was an attractive guy with his blond hair and symmetrical nose. He wore the slacks she'd bought him last Christmas. They fit way better than any in his closet when they started dating. His haircut was compliments of the stylist she'd arranged for him to see. And, not that she was looking, but the tooth-whitening toothpaste she'd dropped on his counter definitely did the trick.

In the game of leave-things-better-than-you-found-them, she'd done well with Tom.

This was little consolation because she may have been the woman who fixed him up, but he was the man who broke her heart. She'd already put it back together with paper mâché and some Elmer's glue, but what seemed to hold strong before lunch now felt questionably gooey.

She'd seen him post-split. They worked in the same hospital, so it was unavoidable. But he'd never sought her out and she'd never tried to catch him, either.

"Hi." He stepped forward, his hands in the pockets of his white doctor's coat—good to see he continued to use the wrinkle release spray like she'd introduced him to. "I… tried to call you."

"This—" She waved between them. "We don't need to do this."

She'd had to turn off her phone because it was blowing up. Later, she'd deal with the messages and sort through the voicemails. But for now, she left it in her purse.

He surveyed her, but her body was oblivious to the perusal. Not like with Mach. Darn it. She needed to stop comparing everything to Mach. He'd made her life difficult enough today.

"Are you okay?" Tom asked. "This whole thing downstairs seems like it's a lot."

"It is," she agreed. "And I am fine. Just… dealing with the fallout."

Tom could go ahead and suck frogs somewhere else. She was ready to go home.

She pulled her tongue deeper into her mouth so she didn't accidentally say something that couldn't be unsaid.

"Mom saw your write-up online. She asked me to check on you," he continued. "She says hi."

"You're here because your mom asked you to be?" she asked, pointing to the carpet.

Tom nodded. "I told Mom it'd be weird for me to check on you. After everything."

He was correct. If there was one thing that could've made this more awkward, that would be the thing.

"Uh-huh." Darla forced a smile. "I'm fine, though. Tell your mom hi, and thanks for checking on me."

She didn't have anything else to say, so she turned on her heel and let her hips sway as she sauntered to the elevator. Tom may have been the one to walk away from their engagement, but this time, she got to be the one who left.

She'd already cleared out her locker into the bag slung over her shoulder. The next stop was the parking garage. She sighed inside.

Then she'd figure out what came next.

She jabbed the elevator button with fierce determination, the bright light illuminated under her thumb. She climbed into the cab and waited while the hum of the elevator's motor kept her company. When the elevator doors opened at the parking garage, it was quiet there, too. She walked with a steady staccato rhythm, the soles of her shoes slapping the cold concrete.

Almost to her car, the flash of a camera behind Dr. Bentley's green Jeep Cherokee burst through the precarious wall of just-keep-going she'd been holding onto.

"Holy crap," she whispered to no one but herself, and took a step backwards, her heart beating too fast.

"I was hoping to catch you, Darla." The camera dude hurried towards her, just like in the movies. But this wasn't a movie. This was her life. "I'm from the *Tribune*."

"No," she said. "You can't." Because this was a parking garage, and she didn't need to add any fuel to any of this publicity fire that might cost her a job.

The publicity fire that Mach had set.

Dammit. There she went, gritting her teeth again.

It wasn't that she was angry at him. She was just mad at the situation he'd created for her.

Maybe this wasn't his fault, but the date had been his idea. His brainchild. And now his brainchild had cost her overtime, and break time with her girls, and the ability to approach Dr. Anthony in person about a Frontline reference. Email and phone calls didn't have the same personal touch as a face-to-face request.

Gah. She needed to do something. Many things, actually.

First thing? Lose this guy. So she waved goodbye as she hustled to her car, and let herself in. Then she made the decision that it was time to go have a chat with Mach. Which, of note, would have been easier had she actually taken his phone number.

She turned on her cell to do some googling, but the pinging started right away and she noped right out of there, tossing it back in her purse.

The only information she had, really, was the neighborhood where he lived.

That would have to be enough. She'd simply go there, convince the guy at the gate to let her in, and then knock on doors until she found the right house.

She rolled up to the gate as though she was supposed to be there—her aged VW notwithstanding. She'd call it vintage, but really, it was just old. The guard leaned out his window, frowning at her through tinted shades. Darn, he didn't have a name tag.

"Hi." She smiled so he could see she wasn't there for

nefarious reasons. "I'm here to see Mach. He's with Dime-front. He lives in this neighborhood. Mach Powers. You probably know him."

Nonplussed, Gate Guy snagged a clipboard. "What's your name?"

"Oh, I'm not on the list or anything." She pointed to the list as she spoke, trying to take a peek, but Gate Guy wasn't having it.

"I just need to talk to Mach," she continued. "He mentioned he lives here. And I'd like to have a conversation with him." About how his life choices were now bleeding into her life.

Gate Guy blinked hard. "I'm still going to need your name."

"Darla." She waited.

He checked the list, which was silly because she wasn't on it. "Last name?"

"It won't be there either, so why does it matter?" she asked, already defeated.

Gate Guy wasn't budging, though. "Still gonna need it."

"Davis. Darla Davis." Not that it mattered.

"What do you know?" Gate Guy pulled his lips together into something that kind of passed as a smile. "You're on the list."

"No way." That could not be. Not at all. "Can I see?"

"I can't let you see the list," he said, as the gate opened. "But you have a good day."

Talk about shoddy security. But while she couldn't quite believe she got right in, it wasn't *her* security, so this was one problem that wasn't hers to solve.

There was one other little thing, though—

"Which house is Mach's?" she asked as sweetly as possible, given her disdain for the amount this guy must be paid to just let randoms drive right on through.

Security here was definitely not paid well enough because Gate Guy had no issue giving her directions to Mach's house, either. If she'd have asked, he probably would've given her the key and the combination to the safe.

The directions were simple, which was how she pulled into the circular drive of a monstrosity of a mansion that supposedly belonged to Mach. She put her car in park, headed up the walk to the front door, and did her best not to be impressed with the details on the stucco finish.

She was here for a purpose, not to admire anything. So she rang the bell and didn't even look at the fancy wooden scrollwork around the doorbell.

Shouldn't they have one of those camera doorbells? That would at least give them a scootch more security since that was clearly an issue.

The door swung open and… it was not Mach.

"Holy shit, it's Darla," Tanner said as a greeting.

"I'm looking for Mach," she said. "Is he home?"

"Uh… out in the pool." Tanner jerked his thumb behind him.

"May I?" she asked, nodding in that direction.

He grinned. "Yeah."

"This way?" She pointed toward the sliding door that seemed to lead to the backyard.

Tanner nodded, and the sly grin was very reminiscent of Mach. Sam came from the room to the right. Her face lit up at seeing Darla.

"I won't take long," she assured them.

What she had to say would take only a moment. Because she was about to give him her problem and he was going to help solve it. And then they were both going to go their own way.

"I am super happy you came by. Mach's been trying to get ahold of you. He's worried," Sam's genuine smile made Darla wish it was totally normal for her to show up at a rock star's house and then hug the pop idol that came out of the other room.

Because she could seriously use a hug right then, and Sam was super nice.

But it wasn't time to harass all the famous people. It was time to harass one particular celebrity. So she headed toward the door Tanner had motioned to before. She didn't have to turn to see that Tanner and Sam kept pace with her because they were right there with her.

"This is so exciting," Sam said. "I'm so glad I didn't offer to pick up the ladies."

Darla didn't know what that meant, and it didn't really matter because it was none of her business and all of that. Deep breath in, she paused at the sliding door, glancing onto the patio.

No Mach.

But what if Mach was in the pool with a woman? And if he were back there with the woman, why did it make Darla feel like she'd finally caught that nasty stomach bug?

It wasn't like she wanted anything more than for him to put her life back to rights. So it didn't matter who he was with or what he was doing with them.

She firmed her resolve and with a quick push of the sliding door, she moved outside… and there was Mach in the swimming pool.

Sure, she was grateful he wasn't with anyone. But that was totally unreasonable and something that she would think about at a different time. A time when she could ponder how their lives were so very different that while she was mid-collapse, he was floating away all his cares.

"I thought you said he was worried?" Darla asked.

"Well, he shows it funny," Sam said, screwing up her face.

The anger Darla had held back began to boil over because, yes, Darla's world was collapsing around her and there was Mach without a care in the world, floating to nowhere on an inflatable pizza slice. Sunglasses on his face. Orange swim trunks covering his ass. No shirt for his chest.

Just out there soaking up the sun.

She blew out a breath between her lips that made a slight motorboat sound.

"This is how he de-stresses," Sam said. "He's uh… he's been watching Datestagram, so he's up-to-date."

"This is how he de-stressed?" Darla asked, the temperature of her blood raising at the sight of shirtless Mach relaxing in the pool.

And, okay, maybe the heated blood was because he was a hot guy. Maybe it was also because she was ready to admit that she was pissed.

Maybe it was other things, too.

There were many reasons a person's blood felt hot. Hypothyroidism and hormone imbalance, to name a couple. She could have a full panel of bloodwork run later to rule out anything medical. But for now—

"I'm so glad he's not shagging anyone in the pool when I need to talk to him," Darla said. Out loud. For everyone to hear.

Her cheeks pinked. *Filter, Darla. That was an inside thought.*

Sam snort laughed and covered her mouth with the back of her hand. "I like you. You would fit in great around here."

"I'm not staying," Darla assured. "But the sentiment is sweet. Thanks."

"You're welcome for the sentiment," Sam said with a little grin toward Mach. "For what it's worth, he's going to be so surprised to see you."

"Oh?" Darla asked.

"Mach's not a huge fan of surprises," Sam said with a glint in her eye.

Darla wasn't either. And was it Darla or was there some kind of underlying girl code thing happening there? Like Sam was giving her information that might come in handy later.

Darla took another step outside. Then another. Sam and Tanner closed the sliding door, apparently deciding to stay inside with the air conditioning.

Which meant Darla had Mach all to herself.

Her blood heated again and her heartbeat was faster as she marched straight toward him.

Chapter Seven
MACH

DARLA HAD GONE DARK, and the hospital wasn't saying a word.

There was nothing Mach could do for the situation. So he did the only logical thing. He went back to where life made the most sense—his pizza slice.

What could he say? It wouldn't float without him. Fine, that wasn't entirely true since it floated all the time without him. But it sure as fuck wouldn't be as comfortable without him.

Unfortunately, no amount of sun was hitting his happy button today. No, Mach was straight-up frowning, and that *never* happened in the pool. This was the place where his happiness was guaranteed.

Time to go inside and turn on Netflix, find something mindless, and see if that worked. Maybe he'd even draft up some lyrics for Linx's new song compilation. That might take his mind away for a bit.

He opened his eyes, ready to go inside, and there was Darla standing beside the pool. He yelped—he did. And he nearly fell off the damn pizza.

She stood with her arms crossed, and her lips moving, but no words came out. Like she was rehearsing.

Fuck, she was cute when she was figuring out what to say.

He pulled his bottom lip under his teeth because he didn't need the sun when he had Darla.

The first thing out of his mouth probably should've been an apology for something. He wasn't sure what exactly, but call it intuition.

But that's not what he did. Instead, he lifted his palms behind his head, threading his fingers together like he didn't have a care in the world before he said, "You figure out what to say to me yet?"

Darla stopped talking to herself and her expression went slack. "Are you for real?"

"Totally," he assured.

"Do you even understand what's happening out there in the world?" She gestured to the world at large.

She was pretty. Like an angel, with the way the sun glowed behind her.

"Hans came over and gave me the rundown. We tried to reach out, but couldn't get to you," he said.

That was the truth, but it wasn't *entirely* the truth. Hans had tried to reach out. Mach didn't. He was too chicken-shit-scared that if he made the effort, Darla would shut him down. Crushing what was left of his ego.

"Everything's a mess," she said, the words wobbly. Her expression crumbled in a way that had him sliding off of the pizza slice into the water so he could sidestroke over to her and figure out how to take that wobble out of her words.

He made it off the pizza, but he didn't get to swim before she heaved a breath and clearly switched some kind of button when she announced, "If you hadn't hit on me, then none of this would've happened."

He drew his eyebrows together. "There are only a few things I refuse to regret and one of them is shooting my shot."

Even on the few occasions when it fails.

"You didn't even want to be with me. I was just in front of you." She swallowed hard, as though worried he would confirm this for her.

"You're kidding me right now?" he asked. "She's gotta be fucking kidding me," he said to the sky. "I asked you to relax a little and let yourself have fun. I did it because…" Because he could see who she was under all of that sass and uncertainty. "Because I wanted to spend time with you."

Instead of swimming her way, he stayed put for two very reasonable reasons.

One, he asked her to spend the evening with him so he could show her how fun it could be to relax, not because he was being a dick. And he took it personally that she didn't get that. Resented that she figured he'd chase any tail as long as it was in front of him.

And the number two reason he would not swim to her was because, apparently, when she talked to him in that tone and got him all worked up with the waving of her finger like he was in trouble, well, he got hard.

Something unacceptable when the world was being a jerk, and he was in wet swimming trunks.

"Are you going to get out so we can talk?" she asked, eyes wide, gesturing to the side of the pool.

He pushed his sunglasses on the top of his head with one finger and willed himself to get a handle on the situation in his shorts.

"Well?" she asked.

"No." He preferred to keep his embarrassment below the surface, *thanksverymuch*.

"So, what, we're just going to talk like this?" she asked.

He lifted a shoulder. "It's working so far."

"Ugh. You are so frustrating." She pushed her palms into her hair.

He didn't want to be frustrating. He also didn't want to embarrass himself. So they were at a stalemate.

"You're frustrated. There's a difference between you being frustrated and me being frustrating." This was a reasonable conclusion for him to come to. "That difference being that I'm not doing anything right now to make you frustrated." His hands fell to his hips.

"I feel like I'm yelling at you." She gestured to the space between them.

He nodded. "I also feel like I'm being yelled at."

"Because you're all the way over there," she said, exasperated.

Darla needed a splash of cold water for a reset. A day floating in the pool would do her good.

But he didn't say this because he liked his balls where they were on his body. Instead, she'd just have to come into the pool with him.

"Come in if you want to be closer. There's another floating slice." He tilted his head toward the cabinet where they kept the pool floats. "A pineapple. Even a unicorn if you're feelin' fancy."

"Why?" she asked like it was a dare for him to answer.

"Because, Darla, you are stressed out. This is a stressful situation we are in." Anytime the internet and social media went rogue, shit got tense. "But we are going to figure out what to do about it, but while we do that, we don't need to make things more stressful. So come on in, the water's great."

"I don't have a suit," she said.

Of note, that wasn't a no. It was only a reason. He quirked an eyebrow because, "Darla?"

"What, Mach?"

"You seem like a person who solves problems. I bet you can come up with a solution here. If not, I have one."

She lifted her chin in defiance. "I am a problem solver. All day, in fact. I fix things. That's why I'm out there trying to live my life while *you* are here just… swimming. Like the stuff going on out there doesn't even exist."

She didn't get it, but today didn't seem like the day to explain why he was the person who precisely understood. The man who had been a kid dealing with all kinds of shit. He'd bet that he understood what existed outside of this pool better than nearly anyone. Yeah, he wanted her to understand that, but today was not that day.

"Would you believe I am a problem solver, too?" he asked.

He was about to tell her they kept extra swim stuff— suits and trunks and anything else someone might need for an impromptu pool party—stocked in the guest bath by the kitchen.

But Darla reached down and pulled her hospital top over her head. Wow, he did not expect that.

"Problem solving in action," she said, tossing the shirt aside.

Serious as fuck, this wasn't what he'd meant. He'd implied it, sure, but he hadn't meant it. He didn't think she'd do it.

Under her top was a tiny black tank. Actually, it could've passed for a full-coverage bikini top, easily. He stared because, well, he was trying to not be an ass, but he was still him.

"You're really not coming out?" she asked, huffing as

she toed off her orthotic sneakers. "You're going to make me come in?" The fire in her gaze made him want to challenge her so she could challenge him back.

God, he wanted her to challenge him back.

He swam farther away from her to make his point with no words spoken.

"If you decide you want my solution, all you have to do is give me the thumbs up," he said. "I do not mind helping you out."

She seemed to get off on the challenge between them as much as he did because with that, she shimmied out of the polyester hospital pants. The pants hit the ground, and she stepped out of them, revealing a perfectly acceptable pair of boy short underwear that covered everything but somehow still made him harder.

Too far, Mach. This is going too far.

"I'm coming in now. Are you happy?" She stomped her way to the deep end, her fists clenching and unclenching along the way.

"Are you having fun yet?" he asked.

"No," she clipped.

But she would be because the water was healing. He understood that. And if she allowed herself the freedom to actually jump in, she'd understand it, too.

Their gazes tangled and the standoff reached a crescendo when she marched to the deep end and, with a grace he didn't expect, folded her palms together above her head and dove right in the pool, kicking her feet behind her like she was born for the water.

Mach was apparently a masochist because, as she swam closer, he realized his mistake in inviting her in as his body ached to reach for her and he didn't mind one bit.

She broke the surface of the water right in front of him, treading water, so they stayed eye to eye.

"Now we can talk," she said, droplets of water settling against her lips and that invisible tug between them even more insistent than the other night.

"We don't *have* to talk," he said, husky and turned on and trying not to be.

What he meant was that they could float together. He could get her a floatation device and he could climb back on the pizza, and everyone could chill.

He did not, however, clarify this for her.

"Why are you doing this to me?" she asked.

Not that anyone would ever buy it, but he played innocent. "Doing what?"

"Pretending to be all attracted to me. I mean, I'm me. It's not like I'm one of your usual girls. *I* get that. So stop making me feel bad about understanding my place in the world."

Now that surprised him. He expected her to ask him why he kept up this game between them. What she said instead made absolutely no sense.

"Your place in the world?" he asked. Was she speaking an unfamiliar language? Because he wasn't understanding her. At all.

She paused and he'd bet she would've crossed her arms if she weren't using them to tread water. "You are a ten. I am definitely not even allowed to be in the realm of a ten."

Last he checked, they didn't put any stipulations on who could be fans of the band. Anyone who wanted to be a Ten could be one.

He squinted. "What?!"

She poked him in the chest with her finger. "Stop it with the hungry looks and the thing you do that makes me want to say yes to your advances."

Holy shit, she was talking about a real imaginary number system applied to the appearance of certain humans by other humans. Which was ridiculous because there was a helluva lot more to a person than how they rated on some fake scale.

Also, she thought he was a ten on that imaginary scale? Damn, he wanted to thank her for the compliment.

But the fact that Darla did not rate herself as high? That was straight-up bullshit.

"You don't think I'm actually attracted to you?" he asked, clearing the air so he wouldn't continue to be a total idiot about this whole thing.

Her chin lifted the slightest of millimeters. "I think I turned you down and I'm now a challenge."

For real?

"Which is fine," she continued. "But don't mistake that for actual attraction towards me. You don't want to be attracted to me. You're not attracted to me. I'm just a box for you to check."

He opened his mouth to say something, but she raised her finger like she wasn't done.

So, what the hell, he shut his mouth.

"But can we deal with that another day? Right now, my job asked me to take a vacation, so I'm not a distraction." She paused, treading water with her arms long enough to make air quotes. It cost her and she bobbed slightly up to her lips, but she recovered just as quick. "I never even got to ask Dr. Anthony to give me his reference in person!" Her breasts heaved as she paused.

Don't look, Mach. Don't look.

"And *then* there was a photographer from the *Tribune* who scared the shit out of me in the parking garage at work when I was trying to leave. He jumped right out and pelted me with questions." She bit at her bottom lip, then pursed her lips and steeled herself. "Don't even get me started on the guy with a nail in his hand who wanted to take me mini golfing."

That was great that she had that amount of control over herself in the water, but hold the fuck up.

"Some asshole cameraman scared you?" he asked. "He scared you because of me?"

She nodded, her finger once again on his chest, but this time it no longer poked him, but just lightly touched.

"That'll be handled. You don't need to worry about that happening again." He'd be dealing with the photographer situation. Oh hell, he'd be dealing with it.

"I don't know who Dr. Anthony is," he continued. "Seems like it's a big deal to you, though, so it's a big deal to me, too." That sounded good. He should write that down so he could use it again the next time he got on Tanner's nerves. "And I have no idea what to say about a dude with a nail in his hand."

Somehow, the space between him and Darla had closed a scooch. Which was funny because he wasn't moving. His feet touched the bottom of the pool. So it must've been her closing the gap.

"About the other thing." He looked down at her fingertip still resting against his skin. He lifted it with his hand and linked them together. Moving so he could take her weight and she didn't have to tread water anymore. "Trust me, Darla. If I *wanted* to be attracted to someone, you're right, it wouldn't be you."

She tamped down the hurt in her expression, but he didn't stop because he wasn't done. Instead, he toyed with her fingers. Fingers she pressed against his.

"That's the thing about attraction, right? We don't get to choose. That's why you've got to go with the flow. Let shit happen."

"Why wouldn't it be me?" she asked with a squeak.

He closed his eyes because he was barely ready to admit the truth to himself. She challenged everything he believed. She made him think. She made him laugh. She made him hard.

He didn't say any of that, though.

"Nothing about you is easy," he said instead. Starting with the way he got all twisted up around her. "You're complicated with a capital C. But the way you argue with everything I say is so fucking cute."

"That's not true," she said. "I don't argue with everything."

"See? Fucking adorable."

They both stared at their still-linked fingers, their chests brushing against each other.

"I don't think you're right," she said, breathy, her breasts brushing against his chest. "I'm the easiest person I know."

"Whatever the opposite of easy is? That's you, Darla." He squeezed her fingers before pulling his hand away and putting space between them. Necessary space, so he didn't do something stupid. Like ask if he could kiss her, so she could shoot him down again.

She looked up at the sky. Then she pierced him with her gaze. "You didn't even check me out. You are like the king of the players and you've never even looked at my breasts once. There. I said it. It bugs me."

"You're pissed that I've got a reputation as a player?" he asked, slowly trying to wrap his head around this recent development. "But you're also mad that I didn't check out your tits?"

She pointed to her boobs. "They're excellent, Mach. Perfectly perky. But you wouldn't know because you didn't even look."

"You honestly think I didn't check out your rack?" he asked, deadpan.

She was on a solid tear now. "Well, you didn't. When we met at Brek's Bar, you were a totally nice guy."

He moved closer to her again, stalking, until his lips were barely a brush away from hers. As expected, she gave up no ground.

"I did," he said with his lips right in the air over hers. "And I liked what I saw, but I was trying not to be a dick and make you uncomfortable by being obnoxious about it, because despite what you think of me, I am not that guy."

"How can I believe that?" she asked, once again defiant.

He glanced at the surface of the water. Cleared his throat. Then he wrapped his hand around the back of her neck and pressed his forehead to hers. "Let's be clear about something."

"Oh, by all means, let's be clear." She brushed her lips against the corner of his, nearly pushing him over an edge neither of them was ready for. Not yet.

"Going in, I thought you knew it was a publicity stunt," he said, letting his mouth brush her earlobe as he spoke. "Thought you were a fan looking to meet a guy who makes money playing music onstage." He breathed in the scent of whatever citrusy shampoo Darla used mixed with the chlorine in the water.

She trembled and held on tightly to his shoulders.

He liked that.

"First thing I did when I saw you was notice how pretty the peach flecks in your eyes are," he said, letting his breath feather against her cheek. "Sorry I didn't check out your girls." Not something he ever thought he'd admit. "But I promise you, when you were walking in front of me, I checked you out everywhere. But I didn't make a scene about it because I wanted you to be comfortable." He pulled his head away, allowing her to take that in.

She gasped in surprise, her lips parting into a little O.

"You can stop worrying about if I like your body, Darla." He grinned what he knew was a wicked grin. "I promise, it's fine."

"Fine?" she asked, glancing at her chest. "It's fine."

If she looked worked up before that he hadn't checked her out, now she was positively in a tizzy. She had the look of a woman ready to kill him, right there in that swimming pool.

"Darla, whatever rating system you've put on the world, stop. That's not a game you want to play with me," he said with a pointed glance that held her gaze steady with his. "Maybe instead let's play something where we can both win."

"It's not that I don't want to play this game with you." The hungry glance at his mouth and the way her lips parted told that story for her. "It's that I can't."

"Why not?"

She gulped. Then she pressed her lips together and wished she could cross her arms over her chest without sinking. "Because that's not how my life works."

Chapter Eight
DARLA

PEOPLE in high school used to call her Dippy Darla since she worked in an ice cream shop on the 16th Street Mall. Now she was straight-up Drenched Darla. The water gently swirled around them, tiny currents winding around their bodies. Her legs moved as she treaded water because he'd released his grip on her.

She looked up at the blue sky again because there was more chance of her catching the sun than finding her happy with Mach. Mach, who didn't take things seriously and who was everything she shouldn't want.

She looked at him, ready to tell him that exact thing. But his gaze snagged with hers and his expression went blank, then puzzled, then puzzled with a side of amusement.

Which was ridiculous since there was nothing to be amused about.

Instead of saying more, or waiting for him to say something else, she did a quick underwater roll, followed by a back stroke, before she came to rest near the edge of the pool.

"This has been fun, but now can we talk outside of the pool?" Darla asked, breathless. She flopped a chunk of hair out of her face.

"I don't know. I'm kind of enjoying this wet conversation." He moved to a back float, his arms and legs wide like a starfish.

She smacked the surface of the water. "Oh, my God. You are impossible."

Mach thought on that entirely too long. "Are you always this worked up?"

It was only a question. That's all it was. And yet, her entire soul seemed to tumble into itself with his words.

"I'm not worked up. I'm happy." She was a cheerful person, dammit.

"I am not afraid to admit that my understanding of emotions is stunted." He shrugged, but this was a pretty big thing to admit, so he should probably take it more seriously.

She couldn't help but wonder what the angle was this time in his statement.

He swam closer again and dammit all, she liked it! She enjoyed being stalked by him so much that she didn't even try to escape. Instead, she allowed their chests to brush again. Only the lightest of touches. But given his admission that he liked her body, she was feeling the power of that admission.

"You were talking about your emotional immaturity?" she asked, tilting her head to the side and tossing up the only defense she could grasp. A defense with a side of sassy.

He chuckled. "You want to know what I like best about you, Darla?"

She shook her head. "No idea."

"I like the fire." His hand barely brushed hers under

the water. Probably an accident. Yet it left pricks of awareness that should have been dulled by the chill of the water.

Often Darla fought for things that had nothing to do with her. Patient rights, and attention for them. She'd burn down the world if it meant her friends got a fair shake. But…

"I think you're right. Maybe I'm not happy," she admitted. "Having fun."

She'd never fought for her own happiness. She'd fought for what she'd believed was love, but it wasn't happiness she had with Tom. He made an excellent project, though.

"What do you want?" Mach asked, the genuine gleam in his eyes breaking through the wall she'd tried to build.

"What are my options?"

"There's always the predictable."

"Yes." She fist-pumped. "What's that one? That's my choice."

"Okay, here's how we do that. I make some calls. People smarter at this stuff than us will figure out how to make this thing with the influencer and the video go away. You can go back to your life. I go back to mine."

That sounded precisely like the option she should select. Yes, that's the one she should take. The safe option. Then she could finish her application and head off to whatever distant locale Nurses on the Frontline selected. Maybe her manicure would totally suck, but at least she'd be far away from the pull of Mach and all the cameras in Denver.

Yet, even as the thought solidified, her hand seemed to drift all by itself to the smattering of hair on his chest. The worst of it was she didn't even attempt to stop it, letting her skin brush against his and those delightful fluttery feelings flow through her nervous system.

"Or." His fingertips barely brushed her elbow. They

drifted up to her shoulder and maybe he'd do that thing again to her earlobe. That was wicked nice. "You take a risk," he said. "Decide to have some fun. See how that goes."

Just so they were clear. "The fun is in the pool with you?"

"The band's headed to L.A. soon for a couple of shows and some recording. Come along. No responsibility. Just time for yourself."

"And, what, I'll just be your personal groupie?" Because that didn't sound like something fulfilling.

The question bought her a Mach grin. "Is that what you want?"

"No!" She was so much more than that.

He lifted his fingertips up along the back of her arm to her shoulder. "Given that you are you, I am certain you will find something to do that will change the world as we know it."

"I don't exactly have the income you have. I can't just leave." Could she? But she couldn't precisely stay, either.

"Don't you have to leave your job anyway?" he asked.

"It's complicated. I mean, the hospital is forcing me to take a leave of absence, so they're paying my standard pay. But there won't be any overtime, which is my Starbucks money. So…" She should cut to the point. "Yes, and no. I need a job. But I also have one already."

He nodded. "Okay. Done."

Hold up. "What do you mean, okay, done?"

"I mean. It's done. You're hired. I'll pay you enough to cover the difference."

"To do what?" She didn't mean to make a squeaky, shrieky noise with the question. This situation was so bizarre, her mind raced, trying to understand how they got to this point.

And how they were still in the damn pool.

He lifted a firm shoulder. "You can do whatever."

"But what's my job?" she pressed.

He blinked as though this was a ridiculous thing to ask. "Anything you want it to be."

That made no sense at all.

"And how much are you paying me to do whatever I want?" She couldn't press her hands against her hips since she was holding onto the edge of the pool, but she wanted to.

"Whatever overtime pay you're missing at the hospital?" he asked. "That seems fair, since it's my fault you're in this mess."

"I won't have anything to do."

He thought about that. "What if I break my foot? I'll need a nurse?"

"Are you offering to break your foot so you'll need a nurse?" she asked. Of all his bad ideas so far, that one was the worst. Just like Tetanus Guy.

"No, I'm just saying that if I break my foot, then I'll need medical attention. If that happens, it's a good thing I have a nurse on staff. Your purpose has been established." He actually patted himself on the back. Right there in the pool.

"When you break your foot, we can have that discussion."

"What if Tanner breaks his foot?" he asked. "That would be more comfortable for me and he sits the whole concert, anyway. No one would even know." He winked.

And this was fun, actually. This conversation wasn't awful.

"You won't have to do anything disgusting." He paused. Thought on that. "Unless you're into that."

She chucked him on the biceps. "No."

"The point isn't what you do, it's that you see how great it can be to have fun."

"Lucky for both of you, I may have a solution," Hans said from the side of the pool, loud enough to break through their discussion.

Darla and Mach turned their heads in tandem.

Hans and Courtney stood beside the pool. Hans in a suit, Courtney in black shorts and a Dimefront T-shirt. She waved. "In addition to being Bax's wife and Linx's sister, I'm the band's publicist. Great to see you again, Darla."

Courtney seemed nice enough, but the title of publicist made Darla leery. One date with Mach was enough publicity for a lifetime.

"How long have you been listening?" Mach sort of asked, sort of growled.

This was a pertinent question.

"Long enough," Hans replied matter-of-factly.

"You two are adorable." Courtney slid off her flip-flops, sitting at the edge of the pool with her legs dangling in the water. Hans didn't sit. He dangled nothing.

"Darla, you are becoming quite the sensation." Courtney pointed between the two of them. "But I guess you already know that."

"What's this solution?" Mach asked, glancing between Hans and Courtney before moving his gaze to Darla in what looked to be reassurance.

"Welp." Courtney clapped her hands. "I got a call."

"Do tell," Mach said, but he now had a don't-bullshit-me expression that Darla seriously got off on.

"The producers for Gumdrop Productions called. They want you two as guests on the *Lately, Later Show*. The one that films in Burbank."

"For real?" Darla asked. Not only because she always watched it. Only partly because she always watched it.

Courtney nodded. "Yes." She flexed her toes under the water. "Anyhoo, they want the band to come do the show, and they want you two to come on and do the banter bit like you did with Bax."

"Why?" Mach asked.

"Because Darla is becoming very popular on social media as of this afternoon. Everyone is talking about you." Courtney paused, apparently to let that sink in. "Everyone wants you to meet your Mr. Perfect, and no one really expects to see you with Mach again. That's the hook."

"Oh," Darla said, unsure of what else to say.

"Hans and I think it's good for the band if you do the show." Courtney slipped her gaze to Hans. He nodded once.

Darla opened her mouth to explain that—

"Darla doesn't want to be in the spotlight again," Mach said, as though reading her thoughts.

Yes, that.

She wanted things to work out in a well-ordered fashion that didn't involve loads of discomfort.

"In my experience, there are a few ways to make this go away." Courtney started counting on her fingers. "You do nothing and wait until the beast calms itself down. That can take a while... unless another big story breaks to take the heat off of you. This will happen, eventually, but you don't get to control that. And in the meantime, you're stuck in limbo. Waiting."

"I don't like that option," Darla announced. She'd already spent the last month in break-up purgatory. The time to move forward had arrived.

"The second option is that you feed the beast, so it'll go to sleep. Burn all the oil in the lamp as quickly as possible. You put yourself out there, do this show. That goes well. Everyone is content and filled to the brim with America's

New Sweetheart and, you know, this lug." She pointed at Mach with her thumb. "They'll be sick of you both and ready for the next thing."

Hans seemed to think through what Courtney proposed. Finally, he said, "As the attention mounts, Courtney and I funnel most of it to the band, away from Darla. Moving the spotlight, so to speak." He grinned. "It'll work. We can do it. Then Darla goes on with her life, and you go on with yours." He paused and it felt like a dramatic pause, for sure. "If that's what you want."

Courtney made a funny sound in the back of her throat at that announcement, but Hans squelched it with a look. Sheesh, that look was one Darla didn't want to be on the receiving end of. Also—

"To make your proposal work, I go on television?" Darla asked. "On purpose. With Mach."

"Why do you make that sound like a dentist appointment?" Mach asked. "The last part. 'With Mach.'"

"I didn't." Pretty sure that didn't happen.

"Eh." Courtney waved her hand from side to side. "A little." Then she winked. "But it's good for Mach to get put in his place every so often."

A loud crash echoed on the far side of the yard. Something fell with a thud and then another someone crashed. A decent kerfuffle was going on over there.

"We're fine!" someone shouted. "Sorry about the mess."

There was more yelling. A few inventive curses. All female voices.

"Still fine!"

Hans glanced that way, sighed, then looked back to Darla and Mach.

No one seemed concerned at all. That made sense,

given the security situation of the neighborhood. Things like that probably happened all the time around here.

"Think on it." Hans slid his sunglasses back on the bridge of his nose. "Let me know."

He turned and headed to the opposite side of the house from the commotion.

"I usually think Hans is the one that never gets flustered." Courtney pulled her toes from the water to stand on the edge. "But then Babushka shows up."

Who was Babushka? Also—

"That was flustered?" Darla asked.

Mach groaned.

"Shit. That's today," he muttered.

He ran a hand down his face, leaving droplets to drip from the edge of his lips.

Don't look at the droplets, Darla. Don't look. Don't look.

She totally looked.

"What's today?" Darla barely got the second word out before an entire soccer team's worth of elderly women sashayed toward the pool. One of them pushed another in a wheelchair. Another moved slower in her walker.

"It's water aerobics day." Mach glanced at her, and he'd gone a little pale.

She didn't know what any of that meant. Then again, her life since Mach moseyed in had been a great big bag of questions.

What was one more?

Chapter Nine
MACH

MACH LOVED HAVING a pool in the backyard. Loved having friends and family who enjoyed stopping by for a dip.

Honestly, he even liked Babushka and her crew using it for their classes.

But.

Babushka and her crew tended to somehow—and he didn't understand how—manipulate him into doing things he'd rather not do.

Case in point? Last week, they'd made him and Hans participate in their water aerobics class. Mach had no idea how it'd happened. One second he was saying no, the next he was moving to the oldies.

"We're going to want to get out now," he said. Dry land was always a safer bet with these ladies. Better footing and less likelihood of them convincing him to stay and entertain.

"We?" Darla asked, lifting an eyebrow. "I didn't say that."

Her unwillingness to give him even an inch was cute as

fuck. Turned him on in ways he'd never expected. But this wasn't a time to be cute. This was a time to run.

"You said you wanted to get out." She got on him about it the second she stepped next to the pool and tossed around her endless supply of sass.

"You have a hankering to do water aerobics?" he asked.

"No." She shook her head, more adamant than he'd expect from a woman who wasn't rushing out of the water.

He had to push his lips together to keep from grinning. *Not one inch.*

He should've been exasperated. That was the logical feeling. Instead, he seriously considered staying in the pool and letting Babushka and her ladies do that manipulation thing that would end up keeping Darla there.

"These women scare you?" Darla asked.

"No," he assured. The feeling wasn't fear. More like self-preservation.

"They don't scare me, either," she announced. "All kinds of patients come into the emergency department. The only thing that scares me is lice."

"Then you are about to meet the second thing that will bring fear into the heart of even the strongest medical professionals."

"There's no way that's true." Her lips pressed into a wry line.

Then she was about to find out. "I guess we're staying for class."

Darla shook her head. "I'm getting out." She stopped, apparently rolling that around in her head so loud he could practically hear the gears turning. "*Because* I want to, not because you suggested it."

Worked for him. Didn't matter what mental gymnastics it took her to get to that point.

"Yup." He swam right over to the stairs because he

wouldn't argue when she made the solid choice. He also wouldn't hang out, so she had the chance to change her mind.

Before he even got to the first step, Babushka sped up to get to them. That was the second the weight of being fucked took hold.

Babushka was a fixture in his life because she was a proud Ten and she and her crew of retirement home friends came to nearly all of their concerts when they were in town. Unless there was a bridge game. Or an under-the-table, high-stakes bingo game. Or a free movie playing at Regal.

"Vhat do ve have here?" Babushka asked in her thick Russian accent. She had a lime-green muumuu covering her swimwear and lightly tapped her fingertips together like some kind of evil cartoon.

She wasn't evil. Not at all. Scary as hell, yes. But for good causes. She'd made it her personal mission to see his friends happily situated and in love.

That was great for them. Made his heart full when they got that.

But he understood his place and love wasn't something that happened to him. The exclamation point to this fact was that Babushka never even tried to find him a match. The closest he'd ever come to a relationship was nowhere near love. Maybe heavy *like*? And that was ages ago.

He understood. Accepted that for some people, that's the way things went. No use feeling shit about it. Like feeling shit about the rain or the sun… not something he had control over, so he didn't need to have a firm opinion.

But.

Something about the way Babushka looked at Darla like she'd just become the next Babushka project made his mouth parched. Pressure built in his head, like things were all off kilter in his system with no real reason. As though he were in an airplane descending for a landing and he needed his ears to pop to make things normal again.

This lack of equilibrium did not bring happiness.

Still, Babushka's question hung in the air, unanswered. *Vhat do ve have here?*

"Vell?" she queried again. "Vhat is happening here?"

"We have nothing here," Mach assured. "Nothing is happening." Not one thing.

He shot Darla a glance he hoped she could decipher. That look being to move ahead with caution. Because if she started talking to Babushka, then Babushka would get her talking more and then it'd be a whole issue. They'd be staying for class and Darla would probably be engaged to somebody's grandson by the end of the day.

He did not want to stay for class.

Interestingly, he also didn't want Darla engaged to anybody—which was not anything he was going to evaluate too deeply right then.

"Just clearing the pool so you and your friends can do your thing," he said. Simple. To the point. And not leaving any room for further questions.

He tilted his head to the towel he'd tossed on a lounger. But Babushka wasn't looking toward his towel.

She stared straight at Darla.

Babushka's eyebrows fell together. "This is the voman from Datestagram. Vhat do they call you? America's 'new' Sveetheart?"

That was precisely what they'd been calling her.

"This is *Darla*. And she's in a hurry to get out of the pool." Mach made enormous eyes at Darla.

"You do not vish to be in vater vith old vomen?" Babushka asked, her gaze stuck on Darla in an assessing sort of way that made Mach squirm on Darla's behalf.

For the record, Darla didn't show any signs of squirming even though Babushka studied her, clearly uncertain if she liked her. Withholding judgement until she determined if they'd be friends or not.

"Not at all. I really wish I could stay." Darla stumbled a little at the beginning, but she absolutely landed the end of that statement without issue.

His chest puffed up with misplaced pride.

"I love water aerobics." The smile she flashed was pure manipulation magic. "I work at the hospital, and I always tell my patients the importance of activities like this." She genuinely looked sad as she said, "Maybe I can come next time?"

Babushka's eyes twinkled. "Yes, next time."

Then something shifted in Babushka's gaze. A different glint in her eye that he'd seen before—when she'd directed it at Tanner and Samantha. And Linx and Becca, too. This time, it made him woozy since she pointed it right at him.

Fuuuuuck.

"You have strong spine. I like strong spine," Babushka said to Darla. "Mach, do you like strong spine?"

Mach skipped the steps and used the edge of the pool to pull himself out. "Love it. It's my favorite." But he knew where Babushka was going with this, and her brand of happily ever after wasn't in the cards for him. So he pointed at her with two fingers, then at his eyes, then at her again. "No funny business. Darla doesn't need your help."

"And you?" Babushka asked, absolutely serious. "Do you need my help?"

"No." The word was out of his mouth before he even had a chance to process saying it.

"Vell, then do not make mess for me to clean." Babushka made big eyes at him. "Or you vill get my help."

"That's it?" he asked because knowing Babushka there

was no way that was it. "You're just going to leave us alone?"

"Unless you make mess." She folded her hands together. "I have other project at the moment vith my last single grandson. But after that is done, you are next on the list." She gave a pointed look to Darla. "If you are still lonely."

He had a thought that maybe he should warn Babushka's last single grandson. But then he decided it was best to keep his nose out of things that didn't concern him. Especially if it meant she was too busy with someone else to stick her nose in his business.

Babushka's friend, Betty Jane, held up her cell phone, stuck her tongue out of the side of her mouth as though she were thinking so hard it was breaking her brain, and started tapping at the screen. She didn't point the phone at Mach, though. Instead, she pointed the camera at Darla.

Then the telltale sound of a camera shutter made Mach cringe.

Darla paled, looking as though she wanted to sink into the depths of the water away from all cameras. He understood that, given she was in her skivvies in the water and her face was already everywhere.

Mach snatched his towel on his way to Betty Jane. He kept his stride light and arranged his expression to one of humor. He tied the towel low on his hips.

Betty Jane's gaze trailed there, as he'd known it would.

"Whatcha doin'?" he asked.

"It's for my Insta. Gonna pin it to the top." Betty Jane was all kinds of smiles.

"You know the rule. No pictures in the pool." He flashed the aw-shucks grin that usually worked in situations where he needed things to go his way. "Let's delete that one, yeah?"

If it didn't work, he'd have to find a second option because that photo wasn't leaving the property—digital or otherwise.

Betty Jane only tittered a tiny bit when she handed him the phone. Thank fuck, it worked. A few swipes to delete the image and he glanced back to Darla, mouthing, "It's gone."

The brief nod of acknowledgment and the way Darla's expression warmed had him wanting more of that. Assurance that he'd done a good thing, and she liked it.

"I see you vill not make mess," Babushka declared, like she was his proud Russian grandma. "You vill do vell."

Darla moved to the stairs, and Mach met her with one of the fluffy white towels he usually saved for himself.

She pulled it around her shoulders.

He didn't mean to linger on the slope of her neck or the way it met her collarbone in a delicious invitation that made him ache to kiss her there.

The older women were all jumping into the pool like they were forty years younger. Blessedly distracted by the lure of the water.

"So the *Lately, Later Show*?" Darla asked, glancing up to him under her umbrella of blonde lashes. Totally oblivious to the way she made him twist into knots. "We're going to do that?" she continued.

"Your call." It seemed risky to put her more out there when she didn't want to be in the lens to begin with. Yet he trusted Courtney and Hans implicitly.

"You think it's the right thing?" she asked, collecting her clothing and shoes.

He loved that she asked him. Wanted his opinion about this.

Of note, Babushka was absolutely eavesdropping on their conversation and not even trying to hide her interest.

He didn't care.

This wasn't about Babushka, so with a nod to her, he led Darla back to the house.

"It's live, Mach. They record *Lately, Later* live," Darla said, to him but also to herself. Because there would be no do-overs if she fudged it.

"I know. Live brings a certain level of bullshit. But I still think it's a solid option." A safe answer without requiring him to fully commit. Since this was the first time since dinner that the air between them seemed to lighten. He didn't want to mess that up.

He stepped onto the concrete path leading to the house, the hot cement nearly blistered the soles of his feet. He did not jump like a cat with a cucumber as his feet demanded; instead he kept his cool and guided Darla to the grass before she could step onto the heated surface as well.

Together, but not together, they walked on the grass. He stepped on the thick, green blades and the spongy sensation seeped between his toes.

Darla moved quickly, efficiently, beside him. Then she stalled. Stopped, totally.

"Okay." She turned, and with her arms full of clothes and shoes, she inhaled a huge breath. "I'm going to do it." She nodded. "I'm going to do the show."

Was the nod for him or for her? He wasn't entirely certain.

"Then let's go talk to Courtney and get settled on the solution." He strode quickly toward the house.

Darla kept pace with him.

"I'm trusting you," she said, and it sounded like both an announcement and an accusation.

He could live with either of those. They were the same thing, right?

He pulled his bottom lip with his teeth because there was no getting around the fact that she said it, but he hadn't earned it.

Yet.

The thing was, she *could* trust him with this. He'd let her down once with the date. It wasn't intentional, but it'd happened.

It wouldn't happen again.

"Mach?" she asked.

"Yup?"

"If we're going to be meeting with your publicist... where can I put on my pants?" She pursed her lips, and fuck all, he was a goner.

Chapter Ten
DARLA

SOMEWHERE BETWEEN MACH'S house and the grocery store, Darla got screwed.

As in, there was a screw lodged in her tire.

Unlocking the door to the car, Darla slid the canvas bags of groceries onto the passenger seat. She'd only stopped in at King Soopers to grab a couple of things.

When her mom and dad still lived in Denver, she would always call her dad for help with stuff like this. So, even though he wasn't close, and couldn't *really* help, making the call came naturally.

"It's hissing, Dad," Darla said into her cell as she stared at her flattening by-the-second tire. The *ssss* sound of sadness was actually a decent metaphor for her day.

"Best bet is gonna be roadside assistance," problem-solver Dad announced. "They'll be there in a jiff."

Mach was right, Darla was entirely too predictable. Playing it way too safe in her decision-making recently. Maybe it was time for that to change. She could take this opportunity to prove to herself she could do something, anything—even fix a flat tire—to take back some of the control in her life.

"You know what? I can do it." And by do it? She meant she would switch out the damn tire herself.

"Make sure they don't send those guys from Colfax. I don't trust 'em," Dad muttered, his attention clearly split now between the golf game on the television and Darla. "Try to get the garage over on South Broadway. They're good guys. Fix you right up. You sure you don't want me to call 'em?"

"I got it," she assured him. "I'm gonna change it myself."

"Have you ever changed a tire?" Dad asked, now a little more interested in the conversation.

"It can't be that hard," she assured.

Dad harrumphed at that, but he knew her well enough to know not to fight her on this.

Her call waiting buzzed and… it was Courtney.

"Dad, gotta go. My publicist is calling me," Darla chimed in casually like this was a totally normal thing for her to say.

"When you're done with your publicist, call Triple A," he said, like this was her usual reason to get off the phone and not totally nuts.

Darla clicked over to Courtney.

"Hey," Darla said like she wasn't pulling up the carpet to search for a spare tire she hoped was still in her front trunk. Excellent news, it was right there where it was supposed to be.

"Got a second?" Courtney asked.

"Yup." She wedged the phone between her shoulder and ear while she pulled out the spare. Look at that, it came right out. Sweet. "Lots of them."

"Why are you grunting?" Courtney asked, her publicist spider-like senses probably glitching and going haywire.

"I'm changing a tire," Darla said, loud and proud and badass.

"Where are you changing this tire?" Courtney asked, slower than entirely necessary.

"King Soopers." Darla heaved the excellent spare tire on the ground next to the flat bummer tire. "I needed groceries."

She grabbed the plus-sign tool thingy and tried to turn the tire-bolt whatever. But the turner plus-sign thing wouldn't budge. She put the head right there to slide onto the round ball things, but… nothing.

Had she done this in the wrong order? Gah, this was not going well.

"Hey, do you know if I jack up the car before or after I loosen the tire-bolt whatevers?" she asked.

Then she realized how that sounded, and dammit, she should just call a damn tow truck from south Broadway.

Except, no, she could do this. She was a licensed driver, and she'd once read the page in the manual, and how hard could this really be?

"Don't…uh…jack anything up," Courtney said. "Hold on. I'm going to grab one of the guys."

Darla held on since she didn't really have any alternatives.

"Darla?" Mach asked into the phone.

"Hey, Mach," she said like this was a totally normal circumstance, they were totally normal people, and there was no flat tire.

She climbed back into the car so she could have this conversation outside of the prying eyes and ears of the general public.

She relayed the issue, and then Mach dropped an f-bomb.

"You don't need to cuss about it. I've got it under control," she assured.

She took a quick peek at the manual in the glove box. Just a quick bit of review before she really got started.

She scanned the text. Easy peasy. Unscrew the tire-bolt-whatevers, pull off the one tire, and slide on the other. Then screw the tire-bolt-whatevers back into place.

No big deal. She could handle this by herself. Like. A. Boss.

"You just called lug nuts 'bobble thingies' and the tire iron a 'plus-sign doohickey,'" he pointed out.

"It's just a flat. No big deal." It wasn't. No one was even bleeding out. There wasn't a shortage of morphine. And, really, the tire wasn't even that flat. It still had a bit of air. The rim barely kissed the asphalt!

"When's the last time you changed a tire?" Mach asked.

"Never." She sighed and tossed the manual on the seat beside her, falling against the head rest. "I should've just stayed for water aerobics. Then I could've floated away on a pizza slice with you while your abs glinted in the sun."

He was silent. Absolutely silent.

"We could've both pretended nothing was happening in the outside world." That sounded nice.

"Darla, did you just mention my abs glinting in the sun?" he asked.

"I did." She sat up. "You know what, Mach? Maybe it is time to get a little reckless in my life. You want me to stop trying so hard to be predictable? I'm gonna do it. It's not like I have to be at work tomorrow."

For the first time in her life she had zero responsibilities. The weight of that felt oddly freeing.

She spread her fingers on her steering wheel. "I'm going to call roadside assistance, and they'll get me sorted. Then I'm going to buy a pint of ice cream and eat it myself while they fix my tire. *Then* I'm going to go to Brek's Bar, even though it's the middle of the afternoon, and I'm going to drink vodka, and *then* I'm going to go buy a bunch of stuff at Dillard's that I can't really afford, and *then* maybe I'll take a road trip without telling anyone where I'm going."

She heaved a huge breath.

"First things first… roadside assistance," she finished.

She didn't like it. Calling roadside assistance was not a badass move. But it was the start she needed to change things in her life.

"Darla," Mach said her name in a tone that should not have been thrilling. Honestly, it should've been scary. And yet, a zing of attraction snaked up her spine at the way he said her name.

"I am roadside assistance."

Chapter Eleven
MACH

MACH'S ABS weren't glistening in the sun because he was on a mission to help Darla. The best news of the day was that, despite her apprehension, it sounded like Darla was ready to help herself have a good time—even if it started with a shopping spree at Dillard's and eating ice cream. If she was really all in on running wild, then he wanted to be her teacher. He figured he'd take her off to Los Angeles sooner rather than later. Ensure she had what she needed in L.A. so she could get her impulse on.

He had a silly smirk on his face because, maybe, just maybe, she might let him lend a hand on her adventure.

"This whole situation with you all twisted up over Darla is pretty sweet," Tanner said, with no consideration for Mach's current inner-self debate about just how far he could encourage Darla in her decision to embrace a little more fun, without her shutting the door in his face and going without him.

"I'm not twisted up," Mach assured.

"Uh-huh," Tanner said as though he didn't believe him in the slightest.

"Is this gonna be one of those deep talks I'm going to regret later?" Mach asked. Not that he'd ever regretted any of his conversations with Tanner, but he didn't like to dig too deep into any kind of emotional shit.

Better to feel emotions without the glare of life on them. Emotions got complicated, uncomfortable, and made a guy itch all over with a rare reaction to something stupid that apparently didn't bother anyone else.

"Dan's gonna flip when he finds out we got our hands dirty and didn't invite him," Tanner said.

Dan was a mechanic and owned Brother's Garage over on Broadway. He was fair, and he was good at what he did. If there was one thing Mach appreciated most about Dan, it's that he taught Mach and Tanner to be the same. Tanner and Mach both learned the ropes of the car repair business before Dimefront came calling. Dan made sure they learned a trade, so if they ended up back in the system, they'd have a way to get out again.

Mach shook his head. "By the time he even gets there, we'll be finished."

He usually kept his truck for mountain excursions on the weekend, but since he'd tossed in his whole toolbox, and he preferred to be super-prepared for repairs, he loaded it up. He expected nothing out of the ordinary, but Dan taught him never to take that for granted. Yet another gem of knowledge Dan learned from tough knocks.

"Sam's totally into Darla," Tanner said from the passenger seat, window down, staring outside. "Throwin' that out there."

"That's good," Mach said.

"Are you?" Tanner asked, serious as a drum solo.

Mach glanced away from the road. He couldn't stop the half-grin; it came all by itself. After all, he wouldn't haul his ass out to change a tire for just anyone.

"Darla's all up in my head. It's messing with me." Mach turned onto the cross street behind King Soopers.

"Seems like you're loving every minute of it," Tanner said with a wry grin.

"You're not wrong," Mach replied.

Mach had zero idea what would come out of Darla's mouth at any given moment. For someone who preached predictability, she was actually a wild card deep down. He enjoyed that it kept him on his toes. He didn't want Darla to stop egging him on and making him crazy. Because when she got going, the energy between them was nothing he'd experienced off the stage. A buzz that made him want to keep playing her games for no other reason than they made him feel things he'd forgotten how to feel.

Made him consider playing new, dangerous games, the kind with feelings and shit. He did not appreciate how she elicited his desire with only a tiny dash of her sass. But he didn't *not* like it, either.

They pulled into the parking lot, and he already had eyes on her. He parked his truck beside Darla's car, hopped down, and went right to her.

"Hey," she said, holding up a bag of peanut M&Ms. "I got hungry. Want some?"

"Thanks." He reached into the bag, grabbed a candy, and popped it in his mouth. He held her gaze with his own in a way that felt like he was daring her to say something. Do something.

But even he didn't know what that dare was or what it meant.

He swore, though, that Darla did. That something flashed in her recognition, and she knew what he wanted even if he didn't.

And because she knew he wanted a rumble? A dash of defiance fell over her features.

Oblivious—or ignoring—the silent standoff between Mach and Darla, Tanner unloaded their floor jack.

"You're ready to try something new, huh?" Mach asked, ready to lock it in so she wouldn't have time to change her mind. "Shake it up at Dillard's?"

She stood taller. "Yes. You are meeting the new and ready-to-roll-with-it Darla."

"Then, uh, you're ready to take me up on my proposition?" He knelt down and went to work with the tire iron. "Head to California with me early and make some waves?"

He glanced up to her, but she had her bottom lip pulled between her teeth. "I…" She sighed. "I want…"

He loosened one lug nut, then another.

"You're great at that," she said instead of answering the question.

Tanner grabbed the handle of the jack and gave it a push. The car slowly rose, the weight shifting off of the bad tire.

Darla tossed a candy in her mouth with a crunch. The candy should not have been cute. If anyone had asked him the day before if he'd be cool with someone eating candy in his ear while he changed a tire, he'd tell them to fuck off.

No, he was a normal person who didn't enjoy people crunching in his ear while he worked. And yet… he turned his head, so he got a front-row seat to Darla's tongue flicking to the edge of her lips.

"Used to be a mechanic," Mach said, wishing it was his tongue there.

"No way. Seriously?" she asked.

"Yeah way. Seriously," he confirmed.

Darla squinted her eyes and gave a sly smirk. "You're telling me you can do more than just change my tire? Like, I'm talking, you change your own oil, too?" She laughed and added, "Is there anything you can't do?"

He chuckled and pulled the flat tire off the car, turning it and pointing at the screw lodged in the tread. "That's your problem."

"That's a little screw to cause such a big issue," she said. "Amazing, isn't it? How the littlest things have the biggest consequences?"

"Or the biggest rewards," he countered with a wink, since the conversation wasn't really about the screw anymore at all.

"Be glad it's not higher up the sidewall." He grunted as he hefted the tire into the back of his truck bed. "Then you'd need a whole new tire."

"Don't I need a new tire?" She looked at him like his elevator wasn't quite reaching the top floor.

"Nah, the tire's still in good shape. Looks like there isn't any other damage so I should be able to fix it up, and it'll be good to go."

"You can just fix it?" she asked, surprised. "How?"

Did he like the awe in her words? Yeah, he did.

"Same way you fix people." He shrugged, wiping his hands on a rag and tossing it in the tool kit. "Skill."

"Huh." She pointed at him with an M&M between her fingers. "Who knew you were so mysterious, with such hidden depths?"

Mach scanned the area, and Tanner was busy with the toolbox, so no one was looking in their direction.

He should've backed away and finished up with her tire. Did what Courtney said to do and tell Darla the details of the *Lately, Later* show appearance she was squaring away.

But he didn't do any of that.

Instead Mach moved slowly into Darla's space, fencing her in at the side of the truck with his body until her eyes glimmered and she was breathing more quickly, the effort making her chest rise and fall right against his body.

This was that dangerous game he was toeing the line on.

"You think it's funny, huh?" he asked. "Don't forget you're playing in the deep end with me."

The M&M still in Darla's hand, he leaned in and took it with his mouth. With the scent of peanuts between them, and the taste of chocolate candy coating on his tongue, he understood he was also playing in the deep end and the odds of drowning in Darla were high.

Darla said nothing, her hand still poised as though holding the now nonexistent candy.

"And, yes," he said, when she said nothing else.

"Yes, what?" she asked with an edge of a squeak to the question.

"I can change your oil," he said and then paused briefly, "I can do a lot of things—flush your transmission, rotate your tires, change your brake pads, and even rebuild your carburetor."

Once again they were not talking about her vehicle.

"Is my carburetor broken, too?" she asked, breathlessly.

He intentionally leaned in closer, so their bodies were only millimeters apart. If anyone looked their way, they'd see nothing but two people having a conversation.

Then he lifted the pad of his thumb to the edge of her mouth where a little chocolate had settled in the crease. "Your carburetor is just fine."

His eyes held hers the entire time that he wiped away the crumb before lifting his thumb to his mouth and sucking off the residue.

Time suspended between them, and there was no forward progression. Just them.

"Want another one?" she asked, holding up the bag,

the hopeful fake-as-hell innocence in her eyes giving him the fix he so desperately wanted before.

He reached for one. Because why the hell not?

The taste of her candy mingled with the scent of her perfume—vanilla and cinnamon, warmth and comfort.

"Mach?" she said, and her gaze entwined with his as she said, "Let's go to California."

Dammit all, but that made him feel ten feet tall. A hazardous feeling because when a guy felt like he was floating on a pizza slice—like gravity didn't apply to him anymore—he'd be tempted to stay in that feeling forever.

"Are you really ready for this?" Mach asked and he couldn't help but grin.

Darla hesitated for a moment but then nodded, a small smile playing on her lips. "Let's release my inner rebel."

Chapter Twelve
MACH

MACH SHIFTED in the fancy leather airplane seat, trying to get comfortable. Failed. Tried again. Failed again.

Fuck it all, he was so tense, his neck was killing him. He rubbed at the base of his skull, but it didn't help.

When Mach went back and forth between Denver and L.A. he generally booked a commercial flight. Getting from Point A to Point B was just as easy on a public flight and it was better for the environment, according to Courtney. She and the other guys flew commercial this time for the "appearance points." That was stupid since there was a private jet going too, but this was one of those Courtney strategy things no one questioned.

But this time he arranged for private transportation so Darla could have the real rock star experience. They borrowed the record label's private jet—all white leather and polished gold. He leaned back, taking in the sheer decadence of the jet, the shiny wood finishes encasing them in lavish comfort. Shiny wood finishes everywhere— including the bathroom.

That seemed a bit of a waste since nobody cared if the bathroom was swanky.

The trip should've been fine. But it wasn't, because Mach was on edge as soon as the landing gear lifted. What was he really doing here and why were all the figurative knots pulling tighter, an emotional noose he did not enjoy? The noose may have been all in his head, but his body's reaction to it was intense and his neck was fucking sore.

Darla didn't seem to notice his internal struggle as she dove into research on her phone to figure out what she wanted to do once they landed with the days they had together.

And all he did was watch her bite at her lip, take notes, then go back to the phone.

Not like a creep or anything. Like a guy who genuinely started to wonder what Darla thought about. What made the same features of her face light with fire and then fade into peace?

Then again, the hope for chatter was more than just a preference for wanting Darla to keep him on his toes. He'd just never been a guy to enjoy the quiet—he'd always slept with the radio on to keep him company.

"Here's what we are going to do," Darla announced from the white leather seat across from him.

"Can't wait to hear." He had told her to go crazy with his credit card since the last time he'd offered her anything at all in Denver, she chose donuts and a blender. He trusted her not to buy five Lamborghinis or a penthouse on the beach. This time she did seem to be more up for the challenge.

"I've got a list of things for us to do—like a scavenger hunt though L.A." Her eyes danced as she held up her notebook, the pages filled with scribbles. "And three guesses how we are going to do it?"

"I have no idea." A scavenger hunt through L.A.? That's what she wanted to do, huh?

"On Segway scooters," she announced with jazz hands. "I found a rental place."

She might as well have announced they'd be doing their tour riding penguins because—

"There is zero fucking way I'm getting on one of those things," he countered.

She pulled her lips to the side. "Well, how are we going to get where we need to go?"

"There are five-thousand better ways than on one of those fuckin' scooters." Mach ran his hand over his hair while he shook his head.

"Oh." She started scrolling on her phone again. "Well, I sort of already rented them." She grinned a flashy white smile. "Too late."

He had become used to the numb emotion of his usual days. Little thrills of excitement happened, sure, but he didn't live in Technicolor. That's why he liked Darla when she threw sass like she was on a parade float tossing candy to the littles.

"Can I see your list?" he asked, holding his hand out and curling his fingers inward as if to say "gimme."

She handed over the notebook, which he quickly scanned. There was a trip to the Griffith Observatory, checking out Mulholland Drive, a visit to the Hollywood Sign—all typical tourist stuff scrawled on the page.

"You're trying to be predictable," he said as he clucked his tongue.

"Not predictable. I'm just making a plan. It's totally different." She shrugged her slender shoulders, then rubbed on some lip gloss and smacked her mouth.

"Can I help you with your plan?" He flashed her what he hoped was an encouraging smile.

"Of course!" she said, eagerly.

"And you trust me to help you with your plan, no matter what it involves?"

"Is it legal?" She cocked her head to one side, studying him carefully.

He hesitated a second before replying. "Probably."

"Then… okay." She nodded her acceptance of his terms.

In one swift movement, he grabbed the sheet with the carefully written lines and ripped it out of the notebook. Folded it up and shoved it in the pocket of his jeans. "The plan is that there is no plan."

She quirked an eyebrow, so it kissed the bottom edge of her bangs.

He waited. Poised and ready for whatever zinger she prepared to toss at him. Finally, she pinched her lips together. "I don't really like that plan."

"Isn't that the point?"

The buzz of the landing gear coming down marked the real start of their adventure. He watched the airport roll into view, excited for the first time in a long time about something other than music.

"How's the water out here?" she asked. "Is the tap good or should we stop for bottled on the way?"

"Water's fine. It's water," he replied, since he'd never given any thought to it.

"See that's where you're wrong," she said, talking with her hands. "Not all water is created equal. I love Denver water, not so much the tap water in Orlando, but Portland was fine when I visited there." Damn, but the way she scrunched up her nose was cute.

"You can have whatever water you want," he promised.

They deplaned and a black Mercedes-Benz drove up to

meet them on the blacktop. Bags were unloaded, they got settled into their seats, and he asked their driver, Rick, to drop them at the nearest new car, truck, or motorcycle dealership.

"No scooters," he clarified.

"Aren't we going to the apartment?" Darla asked, nervously. "It's almost night."

He nodded. "Yes it is, and not unless you want to. Is that what you want to do?"

"I mean, not really. It's just what you do when you land in a new city—go get settled wherever you're staying."

"I'm having a hankering to buy a new car or something." He rubbed his hands together. "You ever get that?"

"Can we do the honest thing for a second?" she asked. "I have a question."

He tapped his foot, his knee bouncing with the movement. "Sure."

"You don't even know what the honest thing is."

Didn't seem too complicated. "I figure it's where we're honest with each other."

"I guess you do know what it is."

He stopped a chuckle and leaned forward in anticipation. "What's your question?"

"Can a person just go buy a car without planning it?" she quizzed, her eyes sparkling with a little sizzle of excitement like she didn't believe it was actually possible.

Without hesitation, he draped his arm around her shoulders and scooted closer to her, drawing her into his side. He looked down at her and smiled mischievously before confidently replying, "Hell, yeah."

She glanced up as he did this, her pupils dilating.

"I vote for a used car, then," Darla said. "You can get a nice one in good condition that won't leave you destitute if something goes wrong and you can't make music anymore."

"We get to do whatever we want," he said. "I have the urge to make a big purchase, and I'm not feeling the pre-owned today."

He glanced out the window as the car jostled over the lip of the drive and they rolled into the Ducati motorcycle dealership lot.

He grinned because this was even better than he thought it might be. He'd figured they'd end up at a Ford or maybe a Honda dealership. But this, now *this* was better. He gave Rick the directions to drop their luggage at the apartment and grab some bottled water for Darla, too.

Then he helped Darla out of the back seat.

"Give me a number—let's say one through ten?" he asked, after a quick count of the bikes in front of the shiny glass display windows.

"Three, why?" She bounced on her toes.

"Left or right?" he asked, still scanning the bikes.

"Right," she said with confidence, her gaze trailing to the same spot where his settled.

"You have excellent taste." He strode forward, shoved his hands in his pockets, and checked out the motorcycle third from the right. Their new ride.

"You're going to buy it?" she asked, eyes wide.

"You willing to ride on it with me?" he asked, studying the way a ray of sunshine fell over her hair like a halo.

She nodded. "Sure."

"Then, yup, I'm going to buy it." He grinned. Then he made the purchase, and they were ready to head out.

Two helmets in his hands, he pointed to her, "Quick. Don't think hard. First place that comes to your mind when you hear the words Los Angeles."

"The beach," she said without hesitation.

He handed over the shiny new helmet he'd bought just for her. The kind with an intercom so they could talk back and forth—change things up if they needed to.

"Let's do it," he said.

Chapter Thirteen
DARLA

YESTERDAY MORNING she'd basically lost her job. Temporarily, sure, but it counted.

Today, she flew down the I-5 on the back of a brand-new motorcycle with her guitar-playing rock-star tour guide.

Was this really how some people lived? Picking a number and then buying something so expensive just to have fun? Even though she was experiencing it firsthand, she still couldn't wrap her head around the reality that this was not a dream.

She dated a guy before Tom who rode a motorcycle. They'd gone out a few times, so she had been on one before. But that bike was nothing like this. The speed and the hit of adrenaline with Mach had her gripping her arms around him, pulling herself tighter to his back. The wind whipping her hair around where it escaped from the confines of the helmet, the freedom of letting someone else be in control, and Mach's strength under her arms—everything together made her feel invincible.

He gripped onto the handlebars tightly, his abs taut

under his T-shirt. The flutter in her stomach was not from the wind or the exhilaration of the ride. No, it was from Mach.

"Doing okay back there?" Mach asked through the headset, his voice kind of muffled.

"Better than okay," she replied, unable to filter out her breathy awe.

He laughed, totally free and without any cares.

"I've never experienced anything like this," she said. "It's amazing."

He chuckled, low and deep. The combination of his chuckle and the scent of his leather jacket with the motor between her thighs was a total sensory overload.

And then her throat went dry as she recognized or remembered that this wouldn't last. A cold splash of water that it was only a blip in the fabric of her life. A twinge of sadness settled in her heart because this adventure would eventually have to end. She would eventually have to go home, back to work, and face reality again. Yes, she understood that. But she smiled, because that day wasn't today.

"Hold tight," he said. "We're gonna turn here."

She did as he told her and exiled her train of thought to another day.

"My mantra is going to be living in the moment," she said. "Especially if the moments are like this."

"Don't settle for less," he said, the words husky. "Never settle for less."

She gripped him tighter as he turned smoothly into a parking lot by the beach, held them up with one leg as he balanced the kickstand, and killed the engine. Then he pulled off his helmet and Darla did the same.

"Yeah?" he asked with a half-grin and eyes that sparkled.

"Yeah," she replied, and she couldn't stop smiling.

With his help she took a deep breath and slid off the back. Her legs were practically jelly from the buzz of the engine and shaky from the adrenaline rush.

"This is way better than a scooter," she said, breathy and gripping his arms for stability. Then she closed her eyes in an attempt to imprint the memory of that ride, and these moments, in her brain forever.

"Mach Powers," somebody called from across the parking lot, totally wrecking the moment between them.

"Well, shit," Mach said, his lips pulling into a low frown.

Darla turned and a couple of camera guys hustled toward them, already clicking away with their cameras.

"Are those real paparazzi?" she asked. These guys didn't jump out from behind a car or catch her right after she left human resources, so they didn't have quite the same effect on her as the dude from the *Tribune*.

"They don't look fake to me," he said, more growly than usual.

Darla waved. "Hi."

They stopped, obviously surprised by her reaction. Then one of them recognized her and it was on. They were snapping photos like it was their job—which, it was, but still.

"Darla Davis," one of them said. "You're here with Mach?"

She glanced to Mach, then back to them… "Pretty sure that's obvious."

"Are you two together?" the other guy asked.

"We're both here," Mach said, and he snagged her hand and tugged her along with him toward a purple food truck at the edge of the parking lot.

"Are we eating?" she asked. "I'm starving."

Mach's hand gripped hers tighter, and she turned to glance behind at the two camera guys still following. She waved again. "Are you guys hungry? We're gonna grab something to eat."

Mach stumbled a little. "You can't feed the paparazzi."

"Why not?" she asked, sort of swinging their hands between them.

"Because then they belong to you, and they'll expect it again."

"I never thought it might be fun to have my very own paparazzi," she said. "I think I like it. I think we should… how did Courtney say it? Feed the beast?"

"I don't think she meant for us to take that literally," Mach said.

But that didn't matter because if they were there to feed the beast, then Darla was going to feed them. Chili cheese fries, apparently.

She and Mach ditched their shoes to walk down to the water, letting the cold wet of the Pacific swirl over their bare feet.

"You might be right," she said as the swirls of salt water soothed her feet.

"Probably am," he said. "What specifically are you referring to, though?"

"The water is healing," she said, looking up at him and meaning every syllable.

Mach's face softened, and his thumb traced the edge of her jawline. He pulled her in for a kiss, one hand in her hair and the other at her waist. His mouth met hers and she lost all thoughts of being sensible. She didn't even have to think; it was as though her body let out a sigh and her mouth opened all on its own under his possessive lips. She let go of any control and let him have it all.

And Mach? He took it—everything she gave. The funny thing was that even as he took it? He gave it right back.

Chapter Fourteen
DARLA

THE PAPARAZZI WERE LIKE ANTS–IT started with seeing just one or two but then they multiplied and kept coming. There were practically a dozen of them by the time Mach and Darla got back to the bike.

They weren't in Denver, anymore, that was for sure.

Courtney had to wrangle some kind of publicity drama with another celebrity over on Rodeo Drive to distract the ants, er… paparazzi, away from Mach and Darla so they could get back to the apartment without being tailed. Mach and Darla had to get really boring, and she stopped offering them food so they could go take the other pictures instead.

So there were no cameras, paparazzi, or social media influencers waiting for them at the apartment building. But just in case anyone still showed, Darla promised Courtney and Mach that she wouldn't feed them on her way inside.

Which was how they made it to the apartment building without issue.

Mach slid the key into the door to unlock the apartment they'd be sharing.

"Irina really lives across the hall?" Darla wasn't able to keep the disbelief out of her words. She had a teeny tiny celebrity crush on Irina—especially after they'd had piña coladas and bonded over donuts.

She studied the outside of Irina's apartment, but it was totally normal. Nothing out of the ordinary.

"That surprises you?" Mach asked, pushing the door open to their place. "She and Knox stay there when they are in town. They'll be in later tonight. You can say hi."

"I mean… I figured she'd have a mansion in Beverly Hills." Darla followed him inside and holy wowza, this apartment they were staying in was all kinds of shades of white. Talk about tone on tone, and pattern on pattern— all of them white.

This must've been one of those fancy-people trends that made little sense for the rest of the world because everyone else used ketchup sometimes.

"What the place needs is a pop of burnt orange on the walls," Darla mumbled. "I miss decorating. That's one thing I loved about having a home."

Mach strode to their bags and tossed his duffel bag over his shoulder as he said, "You don't have a home?"

"Well, not to brag or anything, but I have a room I rent from my best friend right now." Darla made a *whatch-agonnado* face. "The ex got our place when we split."

"That sucks," Mach said. He didn't say anything else, and he didn't need to because it did suck.

The blank-white apartment where Mach and Darla would stay was Courtney's old apartment from when she lived in L.A. From a time before she'd hooked up with Bax, Dimefront's lead singer. She and Irina had been best friends then—and they still were. But in the pre-rocker days, Irina was an actress on the rise and Courtney was the band's publicist. Courtney held onto her apartment for anyone who needed a California crash pad.

Aside from the lack of color in Courtney's apartment, what surprised Darla the most was how ordinary the apartment building seemed. Well-kept with security doors and all that. But nothing that screamed *rockers and movie stars live here!*

"This is where I'm staying." He cocked his head to one of the rooms. "You get the primary bedroom, but we have to share the bath."

Mach grimaced as he headed to one door. He lifted his hand to his collarbone, rubbing the fleshy spot between the bones.

"What's with the face?" Darla asked, leaving her suitcase and moving to him.

"Screwed up my neck," he said. "That's all. At least when we were on the bike, it wasn't driving me nuts."

"Can I look?" she asked, already poised to do just that.

"You won't let me say no, will you?" he asked, eyeing her waiting fingers.

"Do you want to say no?" she asked, because she wouldn't force him to let her check him out unless it was—

She caught a second grimace, and he gritted his teeth. The guy was hurting, and that was unacceptable.

"No. You're right. I am going to insist, because I am a medical professional and there are lots of reasons your neck could be sore. Something as simple as a pinched nerve, or as complex as meningitis." She used her don't-argue-just-do-what-I-say look on him.

It worked because he dropped the duffel and let her palpate his sub-occipital muscles. Damn, they were tight.

No fever by touch, so that was good. But his back was truly a mess—all kinds of muscled knots in there. She manipulated one of the pressure points at the front of his shoulder to help release the tension.

"It'll relax, sorry it hurts at first," she said, palpating the muscles.

He grunted. Then sighed a good sigh. "That's amazing." He moaned as she continued to work one of the tighter muscles. "I think I like it when you make me suffer."

He said the words, but he practically purred against her fingers. He was going to need to lie down for her to really get those muscles to relax.

"Mach." She turned him, so they faced each other so close she got an up-close view of the divot scar on his bottom lip. Time was such an odd thing when they got close this way—like when they kissed on the beach. She'd never experienced this kind of push and pull all at the same time. This must've been that elusive and undeniable attraction she'd always heard about from friends, but never experienced for herself.

"You know that thing we're doing with *Lately, Later*? Where we feed the beast, so it'll settle down?" she asked.

He nodded, and with the motion pushed one of the knots more firmly under her palm.

"Maybe we should do that with us," she said. "With this attraction and chemistry we've been fighting."

"We've been fighting it?" he asked.

"I sort of have," she admitted.

"Do you want to fight it?" he asked.

"No," she admitted, and the air calmed between them. He was barely even breathing. The only movement he made was his chest rising and falling with each inhale and exhale.

She trailed her fingers up his forearm, to his elbow.

He sucked in a breath. "Darla, I'm only human. I can't hold back forever."

She nodded. And the wall was right there, and he was right there, and it felt so natural to do it, so she boxed him there with her body. She wasn't as good at it as he was with her and his truck. But she did her best.

Which was silly because she probably shouldn't have done it. His neck hurt and they were both exhausted from the day. She understood that, but her body clearly did not.

She reached her palms to his cheeks and brushed the beard with the pads of her thumbs.

"Your neck still hurts?" she asked as he seemed to pull her tighter against himself. "You should lay down and I'll massage it."

The hard ridge along his fly pressed against her hip.

She allowed it, even though she should step back and get to the business of relaxing his neck muscles—not brush her nipples against his chest.

"I'm strung so tight I can't even function." He closed his eyes and dropped his head back to the wall, but his hand stayed at her hip and his fingertips made little circles there.

She swore his dick pulsed in his jeans.

"Get on the couch," she insisted. Twining their fingers together, she pulled him to sit on the cushion. Leading the way, she arranged him where she wanted.

He lifted his eyebrows as she crawled on her knees beside him on the cushion, right up in his business so she could get behind and get to work.

"Scoot forward." She nudged him so she could get better placement behind him.

"What?"

"Scoot forward so I can get behind," she said.

"Behind me on the couch?" he asked, clearly confused.

"Either that or you can go face down. What would you

prefer?" She held up her hands. "I'm going to work on your neck."

"What?" He stared at her for a long beat. "You're. Gonna. Rub. My. Neck?"

"Not if you don't move, so I can get into position."

The standoff that ensued lasted only a blip of a second, but it still felt like an eternity. The air thickened between them and then he lay face down.

She straddled his thighs and worked the muscles of his back. The noises of appreciation he made were excellent and by the time she'd worked her way up to his neck, she was hot and bothered and pretty certain he was, too.

This was the part that got dicey. The part where a girl should just confirm that they were on the same page. Yes, he kissed her at the beach. And he had asked her to spend the night with him—but that might not have been sexual. That was more of a "loosen up" invitation.

He'd also said they were staying in separate rooms— which of course made sense because he couldn't actually just assume they were going to stay in the same bed.

Blah, she hated this part. The uncertainty of what came next… what he expected and even wanted.

And, truly, what she wanted, too.

Chapter Fifteen
MACH

DAMN, maybe he should've taken off his shirt? Was that standard protocol for a neck rub?

Fuck if he knew.

But it didn't matter, since there was no way he could roll over with the raging boner in his jeans. So he closed his eyes and figured Darla wouldn't have any issue giving him instructions if she wanted the shirt gone. He'd bet that she dished out directions like a pro once she got out of her own head, and she'd get off on it, too.

That made his body heat even further in entirely inappropriate ways. He needed a distraction or something to take his mind off his dick—

"Right here?" she asked as her hands pressed into the spot between his shoulder blades that'd been giving him shit the entire flight.

"Uh-huh," he said.

Her fingers worked the muscle fibers, and her thumbs pressed into the ache in a way that made his entire body start to relax.

Her hands moved but she didn't stay in one place long

and then the press of her fingers trailed along his spine to his lower back to the edge of his shirt. She pulled it up, exposing the skin, and there wasn't anything inappropriate about this scenario. They'd been in the pool together in a helluva lot less clothing than this.

And yet…

Her hands were on him, and his skin tingled when she touched him. He wanted to moan and make noises that would definitely make them both uncomfortable. His dick even twitched, begging for a little action, but he ignored it.

She used her elbow to follow the curve of his muscle to his hip and somehow when she worked that muscle his neck relaxed further.

"How'd you know to do that?" he asked, as she rubbed circles on his lower back that miraculously also released the stress in his neck.

"My neck hurts, so she rubs my hips?" he said to neither of them, but also both of them.

"The parts of the body all work together. Everything's connected," she said as she continued with the methodical circles.

"No kidding." He grunted as she dug part of her elbow into his lower back.

He practically saw stars. Good stars. Universal alignment stars.

Thing was, he was a normal guy with a standard sex drive, so he should not be worried about nutting on the sofa because she pushed on his back like that. But here he was face down and hoping he wouldn't have to spend tomorrow buying new furniture.

"I'm sure this isn't the first time you've noticed a connection like this," she pushed harder.

He was so fucked because the squeaking noise totally came from him. He wasn't even ashamed because anyone else in that position with her elbow in that place would've made the same sound.

But then she moved her elbow, and damn, his shoulders sighed in relaxed bliss. Somehow through all of that, he was still aroused, and now his neck felt a helluva lot better.

"See?" she asked, patting his lower back right at the edge of his jeans. "It's all about the connections."

"Connections like you pressing on my back to make my neck feel better?" He turned his head so he could talk without his words muffled in the cushions.

"Uh-huh," she said, totally oblivious to what she'd done to him. "You put pressure on one part of the body to elicit a response from another part."

"You know other places?" he asked, nonchalant, like she wasn't rocking his world with her knowledge right then.

"You want a lesson?" she asked, cheerful as all hell.

"Uh-huh," he said, because yes, yes he did.

"Then you should probably take off your shirt." She said it casually, as though this was a normal thing for two people to do with each other on a platonic night in, after days of verbal foreplay and a spectacular kiss at the beach. "I have some lotion."

She stood and moved to her suitcase, turning it on the side.

Quick as he could, to the sound of her suitcase zipper, he pulled his shirt over his head and lay back down, so he didn't embarrass himself any more than he'd already done with that squeaky noise from before.

Darla returned to work her magical spells on his muscles, and by the time she was done, he was a mushy ball of Mach.

He was still aroused, sure, but now it was more of a resigned arousal. Like his dick understood that it didn't get to play tonight, but it wasn't quite ready to give up the ghost entirely.

"Better?" Darla asked, patting his shoulders like she hadn't just rocked his whole world into submission.

"I can't move," he said into the cushion. "I'm going to have to sleep here tonight."

"You want a blanket?" she asked with a laugh.

But he twisted and rolled to his back so he could get a better look at her. During the massage, she'd pulled her hair up on the crown of her head in a clip. She was flushed, her cheeks red, and had he not been there with her the whole time, he would've thought that was the glow of a woman thoroughly fucked.

"What are you staring at?" She frowned.

"You," he said, going with simple.

Going with the truth.

A grin toyed with the edges of her lips. The air crackled between them and he traced the line of her arm with his fingertip.

She cleared her throat. "Do you want to…uh…you know?"

Yeah, he was pretty sure he knew. And, yes, he did want to… you know.

"Is that option on the table?" He lifted his hand to her temple, brushing his fingers through her hair.

"I mean, maybe?" she said, sort of asked. "That's a really crappy reply, isn't it?"

He didn't say anything because that was one of those questions he was pretty certain didn't have a right answer.

"I figure it's just best to ask the question so everyone can be on the same page," she continued.

Then she let her cheek fall against the rough ridges of his palm.

She didn't move. He didn't move.

"I'm so conflicted," she said, falling back, ass to ankles. "I don't want to mess up."

She would not mess it up, he could guarantee that.

"This is your call." He lifted her palm to his mouth and kissed there where her hand and wrist connected. "If you want to rest, then I'm going to take some Advil and crash. If you want to take things further… I'm game."

She bit at the inside of her lips.

"What do you want to do, Darla?" he asked. "This is your adventure." She got to choose what came next, those were the unspoken rules.

"Let's keep going," she said, leaning forward to press a simple kiss to his lips.

He tangled his hand in her hair when he really wanted to pump his fist with joy. "You're gorgeous."

She couldn't seem to meet his eyes at that declaration. But he wasn't giving lip service, she *was* gorgeous.

"I mean it," he said.

"You're only saying that because you can move your head from side to side now without pain."

She was so wrong. So very, very wrong.

"I want to taste you so bad." He held her gaze captive with his own. "It's taking everything in me not to use my loose neck muscles for your benefit."

"What does that even mean?" she asked, rolling her eyes.

He would've preferred to be smoother in his approach, but that wouldn't happen. So he practically crawled to her over the cushions, then pulled her up to him so they were chest to chest.

"This is the time you tell me to stop," he said. "Before I get my taste."

This was the point of no return for him. He didn't fully understand the impact of the thought, but he understood enough to know that once he got the taste, it would change things for him.

She said nothing. Instead, she closed the gap between them and pressed her mouth to his. She tasted like cherry lip gloss with undertones of honey and vanilla, all with a dash of cinnamon. He kissed her slow and let her get used to him before he arranged her how he wanted this time. On her back, facing him.

He crawled over the top of her. His hands clasped with hers and he pulled them over her head, so her breasts perked up to his chest.

He wasn't wearing a shirt, but she was, and that was not okay.

So holding her hands above her head with only one of his, he gripped her hip and dipped his head to the cotton covering her nipples, kissing the fabric.

She arched toward him in what was definitely an invitation.

The pants she wore for the flight were the soft kind with a stretchy waistband. He thanked heaven for yoga pants—easy access and all that.

He kept his gaze on hers, gauging to be sure she was still good with this intrusion as he moved his free hand there to her waistband, then under the fabric of her panties. He didn't go further, waiting to be sure she was still in this.

"Yeah?" he asked, pausing to ensure she was still in this.

She nodded. "Don't stop. Please, don't stop."

He pressed open-mouthed kisses to her lips as his fingers searched her warmth for the bundle of nerves at the apex of her thighs. With his thumb positioned there to rub circles over and around the hard nub, he used his index and middle finger to stroke her open center.

"Mach," she said, his name reverent, like a prayer to send them both over the edge.

With one hand holding hers above her head and the other between her legs, he hadn't touched himself. Hadn't given his dick even a little attention. So when she pressed her thigh to give pressure right there where he needed it, he had to take a pause. Inhale a few deep breaths so he didn't embarrass himself.

Turned out he found something he enjoyed more than bantering with Darla about stupid shit.

He only paused for a second before he went back to work. Then he covered the tight buds of her breasts with his mouth and sucked right through the fabric.

She moaned, and writhed beneath him as his tongue flicked over the fabric, wetting it. She moved against his fingers. She was close.

He wanted to give her this, but he didn't have a spare hand to move her shirt.

So he released her hands and her breast so he could kiss her mouth instead.

Then he pressed firmer at the center of her arousal, moving his fingers inside to the softer spot he knew would provide the push she needed to get there.

Her hands went to his bare back, her fingernails gripping the muscles as her body clenched around his fingers, wetting them more and releasing for only a moment before clenching again.

His squeak from before had nothing on the moans coming from her. And dammit, he was proud of himself. Proud that he could do this for her. If there was ever a woman who deserved a release like this? It was Darla.

As her trembling stopped, he shushed her with soft sounds, stroked her with his fingers, released her from his grip.

"Um… thank you," she said as he pulled himself from her body.

He nodded, but he was absolutely off kilter. He ran his hands up and over his neck, holding onto the muscles she'd relaxed.

"It's your turn," she said, moving to her elbows. "Do you want me to…uh…" She gave a pointed look at his fly and his dick stirred with hope.

What they'd just experienced was the kind of thing that made core memories. It wasn't about… It couldn't be about…

"It's not about turns," he said.

She reached for his arm, gripping his biceps. "We've both got to…so…you know."

The room stopped crackling and everything in him seemed to stop.

"I know what?" he asked, and he did not like where this conversation headed.

Her face fell a little. "So it's fair."

"I didn't make you come so you'd make me come." Because that would make him an asshole and he was, surprise of surprises, thinking he might be done with that part of his life.

"You didn't?" she asked.

And the way she asked, like she didn't believe him capable of giving her something without asking for anything in return? That's the moment his dick understood he was out of the game. That this wouldn't end the way he or Darla wanted tonight.

Because with Darla, Mach realized he was not the guy who demanded favors in return for favors. At least… he wasn't anymore. What did he do with that? If he wasn't who he was, then who was he?

Was it warm in there? Because the room got wicked hot.

"Fuck it all, what am I supposed to do with all these fucking feelings," he said, under his breath but definitely out loud.

"These what?" Darla asked, but the room closed in; the air pressed too hard against his skin. He needed a moment so he could think. Some fresh air so he could breathe.

"All these… the way this feels." He pointed to himself.

"Mach?" Darla asked his name in a way that made him want to crumble and tell her everything he'd never told anyone.

"I'm, uh…" He needed a second. "Gonna head to bed. Catch up in the morning, yeah?" He needed some time in his own brain without her right there, reminding him of what he would never be good enough to have.

"Okay," she said, her expression going blank.

So he did what he promised himself he'd never do again.

He grabbed his shirt, and he left alone. Closed his bedroom door and dropped his head against the wood, uncertain of who he even was anymore.

Chapter Sixteen
DARLA

SO THAT HAD HAPPENED. Mach gave Darla the best orgasm of her entire existence without even taking her pants all the way off. She changed into her pajamas—nothing special, just an old T-shirt and boy shorts. Now she sat cross-legged on the bed in her room, texting with her friends. Hoping they might have a better understanding of what the heck happened.

Patrice: He bolted!?

Honestly, if there'd been a chair there, he'd probably have tripped over it in his rush to get away from her. That didn't feel good at all.

Darla: To his bedroom.

Patrice: Well, that's promising. He didn't go get a hotel.

This was true but still…

> Darla: I have to look at him again. What do I
> do in the a.m.?

What did a girl do when the guy she was on an adventure with gave her an orgasm with only his hand and a smoldering gaze?

> Renata: Ask for another O if he's still
> handing them out.
>
> Patrice: Talk to him about it.
>
> Renata: Don't do that. Horrible idea, dudes
> don't like to talk about stuff.
>
> Patrice: Then trust your gut.

That was the crappy part—Darla didn't know quite what her gut was saying. Not when everything got all muddied from rubbing his back and, well, the other part, too.

> Renata: What if you rolled with it? Kept
> going on this adventure he's pulling you on
> and didn't overthink?

Well, now, Renata just sounded like Mach.

> Darla: Have you met me?
>
> Patrice: I think you got under his skin.
>
> Renata: And I think he likes you!
>
> Patrice: But he didn't want to like you this
> much.

This was all conjecture and Darla preferred to work in facts. Because facts were predictable—they didn't change.

Darla: This is a stretch.

Patrice: But is it?

Darla seriously didn't understand what had happened on the couch, but her gut said that neither did Mach. This thing—whatever it was—between them was burning bright enough to scare anyone. Everything felt new for her, too, and new could be frightening. Clearly, it was this way for Mach, as well. With his declaration on feelings before he left, something told her that he was trying to roll with it, but the spiderweb of emotions tangled him up.

Darla: What if he was only being nice to me and didn't really want to have sex?

Patrice: No.

Renata: You don't give yourself credit.

Darla:…

Patrice: Are you gonna try to fix him?

Renata: Noooooo

Patrice: That's a bad idea.

Darla: He dresses great, smells fantastic, amazing career, super white teeth…what's there to fix?

Like a lightning bolt, it hit her upside the head that she'd been looking at this whole thing through the wrong lens. He didn't need fixing on the outside; he needed help figuring out the inside.

That was it. That's what she could do for him.

Lucky for Mach, she was very much in touch with her

emotions and feelings, and she could help him do the same. Feelings came and then they left, and you only had to ride the wave through them. When you were in the middle of the story you couldn't see the end, but there always was an ending. That was the predictability.

If he was showing her how to have an unplanned adventure, maybe she could show him how to really feel everything and not get overwhelmed by the intensity of the sensations.

Renata: Any word from Frontline?

Darla: No. They said a couple of weeks.

Patrice: Are you ready to withdraw your application yet?

No, she wasn't. She'd need something new to keep her fulfilled once the end came to her time in California.

Darla: No. And I'm gonna go to sleep now.

She was going to try, at least. There would likely be little sleep happening for her tonight.

Renata: 'night

Patrice: Keep us posted.

Renata: With lots o' details.

Darla really didn't sleep great, tossing and turning all night. So she was up early, showered, fixed her makeup and hair, got dressed in a simple pair of jeans with a tank top that would look good if she and Mach attracted more paparazzi, and then sorted through the kitchen to figure out what she could whip up for breakfast. Unfortunately, this kitchen was not an ingredient kitchen—it was a frozen meals and cereal in the pantry kind of kitchen.

Lucky for Mach, supermarkets delivered early in their part of Los Angeles, so she was flipping pancakes when he emerged from his bedroom. The fact that he woke up looking as deliciously yummy as he did was the epitome of unfair. He wasn't wearing a shirt, which was *very* nice. And the shorts he wore left little to the imagination, which was even nicer.

"'Morning," she said, cheerful and hoping to broadcast that she wasn't upset with him leaving her alone last night —but that was a lot to stuff into one word.

"G'morning," he said, his gaze studying her, then the pancakes, then back to her.

"I made breakfast," she announced, holding up the spatula.

"I see that," he said, and he was blinking like she was a mirage, and he was trying to make his brain work.

"Shower or eat first?" she asked, intentionally avoiding any mention of last night or his evacuation so he wouldn't get skittish.

His eyebrows fell together, and he moved to the coffee pot to pour himself a cup. "Food."

She flashed a smile and plated the pancakes for him, tossing on a couple slices of bacon, then sliding the plate to one of the spots with a counter-height stool.

He started in on the pancakes, took a bite, chewed, swallowed, and looked right at her. "I fucked up last night."

She gnawed at the inside of her lips.

Oh no, no, no, no… had she misread it and he really did feel forced into doing what they'd done? A blanket of heavy disappointment started to settle on her shoulders. "You mean the part where I…and you…and then only I…"

He pressed a hand on his hip, one leg on the bottom bar of the stool, one on the ground. He shook his head. "No. The part where I jetted."

Oh, thank God.

She pinched her lips together, so she didn't say that out loud.

"It's okay," she said, instead. "It was a really long day. And super fun, really. I mean, I don't think I've ever had that much fun condensed into such a small bit of time."

He caught her gaze with his, tangling them up together. "It's not okay that I left you like that, and I'm sorry."

Well, since he brought it up…

"Do you want to talk about it?" she asked.

He looked at her like she'd been snorting baking powder while fixing breakfast.

"You don't want to talk about it," she confirmed. "No worries. Apology not necessary, but accepted."

The blanket of disappointment then turned to an unacceptable sheet of awkward as they picked at their pancakes.

"I gotta be honest with you, I'm not good at the touchy-feely shit," he said, finally.

"Well, I'm not good at 'rolling with it' so I guess we are both imperfect." She poked at her pancake with the tines of her fork where the maple syrup pooled.

"Last night felt important," he said, his jaw clenching. "When I try to understand heavy emotions like that, I freeze. It's like it becomes this constant state of discomfort, you know? But then last night I got comfortable…"

"And that made you uncomfortable?" she asked cautiously.

He nodded. "Hey, it's who I am. I guess I'm cool with it."

She hated that she was part of what made him so uncomfortable. Hated that he'd given her everything and she'd given him… pancakes this morning.

"Clean slate for today," she announced, smacking a hand on the counter. "What do you say?"

He lifted his eyebrows, his fork raised to his lips. "Clean slate?"

"Yeah, what happened yesterday happened. We can't change it, so we start over today fresh. No regrets and no looking back."

He let out a relieved sigh, ran his hand over his hair. "I think you might be getting too good at the roll-with-it game."

She took her plate to the stool beside him and settled there, then she said, "I'm hoping today the game involves more major purchases and checking things off my imaginary bingo card."

"Why the hell not? Let's check the spaces and fill that baby up." He smiled at that. "Quick, don't think: up or down?"

"Um… up," she replied, taking too long because she did actually mull that over for a quick moment.

"Spinning or not?" he asked.

"Spinning," she replied, faster this time and without thinking about it first.

"Dog or fish?" he asked.

"Dog," she replied, because who wouldn't pick the dog?

"Done," he agreed with a sly smile that had her excited for what came next. "Let's roll."

And that's how they found themselves eating hot dogs for lunch, 13,000 feet over the Pacific Ocean, in a shiny silver helicopter. The rush of the wind, the sound of the helicopter blades slicing through air, and the sight of the ocean rolling underneath them was invigorating and unlike anything she'd ever experienced. She'd thought Mach's motorcycle was an adrenaline rush, but it had nothing on this.

For miles, there was nothing but the shimmering ocean, interrupted only by small waves. The sun sparkled off the water and cast a dazzling otherworldly light across everything. Sort of like this whole experience with him.

As with all kickass things, it had to end. They landed, and when the helicopter blades came to a stop, Mach helped Darla to the asphalt. A dozen paparazzi clicked away from behind the fencing surrounding the helicopter pad.

Two of them were the same from yesterday so Darla gave them a jaunty wave.

"One sec," she said to Mach.

"You're gonna feed 'em again, aren't you?" he asked.

She nodded and then she skip-walked to the camera guys. She pulled out a handful of granola bars from her bag.

"Anyone hungry?" she asked, as she pushed the bars one by one through the chain-link fencing. Today, they wanted the paps to follow them around for a while so no one said she couldn't give them treats.

Honestly, yesterday's excursion had netted them excellent placement on multiple tabloid websites. The beast was being fattened up before it hibernated forever. And, since Darla had literally fed the guys chili-cheese fries, the paparazzi were really nice to her in the captions to the photos this morning.

"What's your favorite tourist spot in L.A.?" she asked one of the guys from yesterday. "Other than the sky since we already did that."

"Walk of Fame," the guy responded without skipping a beat. "Always love that stretch."

"Darla," Mach called, "Time to head out."

"See you there?" she asked the guy.

He nodded and she was all grins as she sauntered back to Mach because she knew exactly where they were headed next.

Chapter Seventeen
MACH

MACH NEVER EXPECTED there'd be a day when he didn't try to ditch the paparazzi. But today was that day, and he went slower than he'd like on the bike so they could get their fill of pictures. He didn't like going slow and he didn't enjoy being tailed. But he did love having Darla wrapped around him.

It was going to suck when this was over.

When something felt too good to be true, he'd learned not to trust it. And this was definitely in that category.

Even now, with the Dimefront fantasy he got to live, he knew eventually they'd go their own ways and he'd be on his own. Good things didn't last for Mach, and that was fine. It's how things were. It's why he lived the way he did and savored the time he had. He didn't need to think about this stuff too hard because that defeated the purpose of savoring the moment and rolling with it.

He slid into a spot for motorcycle parking on Hollywood Boulevard and cut the engine. He helped Darla off the bike, even though she was becoming a pro and didn't really need his help anymore.

He liked the way she looked up at him with those gorgeous peach-flecked eyes as he helped her down, though.

Darla didn't waste any time once she was steady on the asphalt, heading right to the first star in front of them.

"Stevie Wonder," she announced, and she sang one of his songs—the one about saying I love you on the phone. Huh, Darla couldn't hold pitch at all.

She didn't care, though, that she couldn't sing; she went all in and sang anyway.

"Whatchathink?" she said when he approached her and couldn't wipe off his grin.

"That was somethin'," he said, since it was a safe reply.

"Oh, come on." She linked her arm with his. "Everybody has to start somewhere."

She wasn't wrong and the plethora of street performers down here punctuated her point. A guy near the Roosevelt Hotel played guitar and, actually, he sounded good. The guy *was* good. Total rocker looking for his big break. He sat on a stool beside his open guitar case with an electric guitar and a small amplifier. Dude was young, maybe his early twenties, and he looked like Linx with his wild mane of unkempt hair that fell over his face whenever he bent down to stroke the strings of the guitar.

Mach and Darla stopped for a second and listened, Darla tucked up against Mach's side while the guy covered a Dimefront classic.

Mach reached into his wallet and pulled out a fifty, dropping it in the case. Dude lit right up and put more effort into the song.

"He'd lose his mind if he realized who you are," Darla whispered, her lips brushing against his ear.

"Some secrets should stay secrets," he replied.

"Then we should probably move along before our

camera friends show up," Darla said, all cheeky like she was prepared to go in on a secret with him.

The paps had to park and that was more of a chore than one might think down here with all the tourists.

They continued down the boulevard, the paparazzi finally catching up to them. On the one side was the Walk of Fame filled with pink stars on black stone that stretched for over a mile. Icons celebrated and immortalized forever; it made him feel small but inspired. On the other side of the street was a line of shops and hotels with anything a person could want. Boots and liquor alongside kitschy stores with celebrity bobbleheads and keychains shaped like the movie clapboards they used to call "action."

"You need to be a bobblehead," Darla announced, turning so they were facing each other but still moving. This meant she was walking backwards. He kept his eye out so she wouldn't biff it on a sidewalk lip or something.

"I'm good," he said, but it was nice she thought that'd be sweet. It would be sweet, but he was good and he didn't need a bobblehead.

"I'd totally be a bobblehead if I could be," she announced as they continued on. "They don't make them for nurses, though." She shrugged.

The paparazzi got distracted by some celebrity across the street and stopped tailing the two of them so closely. Which gave them the chance to just be Mach and Darla.

Some spots with the stars were clean, and the air smelled like sunscreen and coconut, with the palm trees as an accent to the backdrop of tourism. Other corners were covered with graffiti or had makeshift tents set up between doorways and alleys. All mashed up together, it didn't make sense.

That was life, wasn't it? You had it or you didn't, and when you didn't, people pretended you didn't exist even if you were right in their face. He swallowed the lump in his throat because he'd been there—he'd been the one who was forgotten.

"You okay?" Darla asked as they passed another touristy trinket shop and she stopped to check out their selection of T-shirts on a rack out on the sidewalk.

He nodded.

"You're not okay," Darla said, and she pulled his arm, so he'd come closer.

"It's just crazy to see how obvious the differences in experiences are like this. It's like you see what you want to see and ignore the rest," Mach said, tilting his head toward one of the makeshift encampments.

"There's definitely a contrast in what people have," Darla agreed. "But people are people. That's the thing you can't forget. I mean, I see people come into the hospital all day long from all parts of life and the one thing they have in common is their humanity when they're hurting. It's why I do what I do, you know?"

She moved her hand along his forearm to his palm, linking their hands together.

He nodded. "I...uh..."

He ached to tell her where he came from, but he stopped because he couldn't. No matter what she'd said before, most people looked at you different when they realized you came from nothing.

"You gave that guy back there a fifty. I bet it totally made his day," Darla said. "And you've been making my day for two days straight."

"I guess I've started a streak," he murmured.

She nodded, and they continued down the boulevard where so many greats had walked before. When she had every reason to be mad that he left so quick last night, here was Darla, not holding his screw-up against him like she should've. The batshit part was that he was starting to trust these parts of himself with her.

"Whatcha thinking about now?" Darla asked, her hand still linked with his as they moseyed down the sidewalk, checking out the names on each star.

"That you make the best pancakes I've ever eaten in my life," he said, since that was a safer thing to say than anything else in his brain.

"It's the sour cream," she said with a half-smile. "My not-so-secret ingredient."

Nah, he was pretty sure it was her company that made breakfast so fantastic.

And what scared the shit out of him was how natural it was to just be in the same place with her like this. Not talking or arguing, just ready for her arms to wrap around him so they could race off to the next adventure.

"I bet someday you'll get your own star, can you even imagine?" she said, studying one of the older ones for an obscure celebrity he wasn't familiar with.

"Nah, no one wants to give me something like this," he said.

Her face fell. "Why would you say that?"

"It's who I am." No sense being upset about it.

"Who is that, Mach? Who are you?"

He swallowed hard and wanted to tell her all about him.

But if he did that, then it'd be over before they even made it to Alfred Hitchcock's star.

"I'm the backup guy. The one in the periphery," he said. "They don't give us stars. Maybe Dimefront the band, someday. But not Mach Powers the guy."

"Nope." She shook her head, adamantly, and started talking with her hands. Practically painting the picture for him. "I can see it now. You'll get a whole ceremony and

Dimefront will all be here to celebrate *you*. Hans and Courtney will have it all planned out and I'll bring my paparazzi friends because they'll want to eat," she said, grinning and gesturing to where everything would happen. "I bet your parents will even come. And brothers and sisters? Do you have any? I feel like I know you so well, but I don't really know anything about you." Her eyebrows fell together.

His heart felt like lead, but this was his reality and he'd accepted it a long time ago. "I don't remember my mom and dad, they died when I was little. They won't be able to make it to any imaginary ceremonies, no matter how awesome you pretend them to be. But I've got Dan—he's my foster dad. He'll wanna be there at your pretend ceremony. The only brother I've got is Tanner and he was my foster brother, so, not quite the real deal." In the blood relation sense, at least.

Darla's expression went soft. He hated that, because he didn't need sympathy. This was just how it was in his reality, no big deal.

"I'm so sorry," she said—the same thing everybody said when the topic came up.

He'd had lots of practice with this, and the easiest thing to say in response was always, "Thanks."

Because if he said anything else it opened him up to more questions and it was none of their damn business. But, then again, this was Darla. And they'd only known each other for half a second in the grand scheme of things, but it also felt like they'd known each other forever, too.

"*You* can ask me about it," he said. "If you want."

She seemed to understand what a big thing this was, and he waited for her to ask away. But she didn't. Instead, she hauled his ass into another souvenir shop and bought a

Hollywood snow globe with the Hollywood sign right there in the center.

They headed back to the bike ready to head off on the next phase of this adventure when he caught the guitar guy from earlier out of the corner of his eye. He was still there, his fingers still strumming across the strings like they had before. There was something special about him that made Mach believe he could be somebody someday if someone noticed him.

He pulled on Darla's hand and eyed the guy. "Do you mind?"

Darla shook her head and followed him.

"Hey, man," Mach said. "You can seriously play. You got a name?"

"Hey, Fifty," Dude said. "Thanks, and it's Sawyer."

"Fifty?" Darla asked.

"'Cause he gave me a fifty," Sawyer finished with a shit-eating grin.

"I'm Mach." He held out his hand. "I play for Dime-front, yeah?"

The guy lit up like a sparkler and the air of casual confidence disintegrated.

"Holy shit." He pushed his hair out of his face and stumbled to stand up. Not because he seemed drunk or anything, his feet just got in the way.

Mach understood that—the tripping over yourself because you got excited. He just never thought it'd happen because somebody met him.

"I thought you looked familiar." He eyed Darla. "And you're the girl from the tabloids. This is wild, you know this guy plays the guitar so smooth it's like butter." He gestured to Mach.

That's a compliment Mach hadn't received before.

"You two should play something," Darla suggested, and

the suggestion definitely felt more like a nudge.

"Yeah, man, totally," Guitar Dude pulled the guitar over his head and handed it over to Mach.

"So, Sawyer, huh?" Mach asked, strumming the guitar and getting a feel for the strings. Every guitar was different, felt heavier or lighter than the others. They all had their own personality.

"Sawyer Mitchell," Sawyer replied.

"Yeah, that's not gonna work," Mach said, pinching his lips together. "You're gonna need something that screams rocker."

"It's all I've got." Sawyer lifted his hands in apparent surrender.

"What about Strummer Sterling? Play it up, you know? Lean into the music," Mach said, still learning the language of this guitar.

"No kidding?" Strummer said. "You just gave me a stage name? This is so wild. I love it. Thanks, man."

"Do you have a stage name?" Darla asked Mach, eyes wide. "Is Mach not your real name?"

He nodded. "Nobody really wants to hear a guy named Mark Flowers play guitar, do they? I fixed it up. Made it better."

"I dig it." Strummer nodded.

"Name the song," Mach said. And Strummer glanced to Darla and then picked one of the Dimefront ballads Bax wrote for Courtney. Mach hit chords and they sang together, their voices melding into a harmony that was not bad at all. The melody was full of emotion as they worked it together.

A crowd formed, and it was awesome.

The whole time he sang, and the people gathered, Mach stared right at Darla. The words may have been written for Courtney, but for him they were all Darla.

Chapter Eighteen
DARLA

MACH SERENADING Darla on Hollywood Boulevard like he was a street performer was the single most sexy thing she'd ever experienced in her life. He and Strummer exchanged numbers so they could jam again someday, and he and Darla were off again. This time he took her back to the apartment, said he figured they'd order in.

"Italy or India?" he asked as soon as they were through the door.

"India."

"North or South?" he asked.

"South."

"On it," he said. "Indian food from the place south of here. Any special requests?"

"Nope," she said, because this was the best way to decide, she'd learned. Let the decision make itself.

Mach ambled off to make their dinner order, and Darla went to her bedroom to put on pants that didn't require a button or constriction. When she got back to the living room, Mach stood there at the counter, apparently waiting for her. He'd opened a bottle of champagne she hadn't seen there that morning.

The silence stretched between them like a rubber band. She wasn't sure if it would break and they'd end up going their own directions, or it'd snap and pull them back together.

"Dinner will be about an hour," he said, his eyes warm and welcoming. "Figured this'll get us by."

"Fantastic," she said, not moving because what was she supposed to do here? Go to him? Go to the champagne? Go to the sofa and sit?

"Are you comin' over here or what?" he asked, his eyes smoldering and hand reaching for her.

She went right over there to him.

He pulled her against his chest, holding her head there to his heart like she was special. Then his hand totally went to her ass.

"Celebrating something?" She eyed the bottle of champagne.

"We can celebrate whatever we want. What do you want to celebrate tonight?" he asked, his voice rough.

"You making me come harder than I've ever come in my life last night," she said without even filtering it a little.

He laughed. Straight up, he laughed. Then he pulled her closer. "What am I gonna do with you?"

"I can think of a couple things." That came out entirely more suggestive than she'd planned.

She'd only been thinking that they could go to his bedroom, or her bedroom, or they could drink the champagne and make out. But the way the words sounded? Well, they sounded more creative than that. A promise she was pretty certain she couldn't live up to.

The rubber band didn't break. No, instead, it pulled them together, and he pulled her to the sofa. She straddled his lap, because she could, and that's where he'd settled her.

"Spend tonight with me?" she whispered against his mouth, nipping at his lips. Using the same words he'd used on her the night at Brek's Bar.

"Only if you tell me what you want me to do." He stared at her lips.

Was that a dare? Because it sorta felt like a dare.

"Table or wall?" she asked, throwing his game right back at him.

"Wall," he said, and his pupils dilated even more.

"Have you ever had sex against a wall?" she asked. Then she didn't wait for him to answer because she didn't really want to know. "I haven't."

"Tell me more about what you want me to do against this wall." His hands framed her face as he tilted his head and kissed her. Loads of tongue and a great deal of heavy petting had her wound up super fast.

"Um…" How was she supposed to know when she'd never actually done it that way?

"You want to wrap your legs around my hips, so your tits are in my face?" he asked.

Okay, yes, sure, she could do that. It sounded super fun.

She nodded. She gulped. Her mouth went dry and between her legs was oh-so-soaked.

"You want me to put my mouth on 'em?" he asked, his beard brushing against her cheek and his tongue licking at her earlobe. "While I hold your ass and you take all of me inside you?"

"You're better at this than I am," she admitted, already totally wound up.

She didn't mind at all, because he could talk dirty to her all day long if this was how that played out.

"You'll learn quick," he assured. "Just tell me what you want me to do first."

"Shirt or pants?" she asked.

"Shirt," he said, slowly, like they had all the time in the world.

"Then take off your shirt," she said way too quickly.

He released her, which she did not like. But then he pulled off his shirt, which she very much did.

"And your pants second," she directed her gaze to his pants.

Slowly, he unbuckled his pants and shucked them off, so he only stood there in his skivvies.

Mach wasn't a gym rat, but he was total masculinity in human form. His thick thighs and defined abs. The smattering of hair across his chest that trailed in a V down to his—

"Now take off my shirt," she said, lifting her arms so he could do it more easily.

Lucky for him, she'd already changed, so there was no bra underneath. With a deft quickness, he removed her shirt, and with one knee on the sofa, he pulled her to him and pressed his mouth to her nipple.

The no-bra bit was actually lucky for her, not him, because he lavished her breasts with kisses. He traced her nipples with his tongue—the whole time holding her in place so she couldn't move. Not that she would've moved away from the amazing things he could do with his mouth.

Her hands in his hair, she said, "Take off my pants."

She'd never had sex like this. She'd always asked for what she wanted, yes, but she'd never had a partner who anticipated her needs and didn't make her wait. Mach slid her pants and panties down her thighs, over her knees, and with a tender touch she could never have expected from him, he helped her step out of them.

There was no more chance to give any more direction because he lifted her to the sofa without delay, and she was horizontal on her back, her knees over his shoulders, his face between her thighs.

She gasped as he licked and tested the sensitive skin there before he dove in and devoured her.

In her experience, this was not the thing men usually loved to do, so if she wanted to ask for it, she had to bake a cheesecake first to sweeten the deal.

Mach, however, was all in. He used his fingers and his tongue until she bucked against his mouth, demanding more and craving release.

"You're going to wait until I'm ready," he said, talking to her between her legs and stroking the triangle of hair where her thighs came together.

"Okay," she said, automatically, but he didn't seem to be talking to her.

"I'm not ready yet." He continued stroking, and swear to God, he dirty-talked to her lady bits like they were a sentient part of this encounter.

That only turned her on more and her hands went to his hair, rubbing his scalp like she'd done on his back the night before. He pressed a kiss at her bundle of nerves, then flicked it with his tongue and nipped softly with his teeth.

Hold up, were they allowed to do that? She'd always been told absolutely no teeth during oral activities.

But he did it again, and… Oh God, yes, he was most definitely allowed to do that.

He kissed her again, open-mouthed, using his tongue inside her to do things she didn't know the human body could do.

She didn't come, but she was so close when he lifted off of her and pulled her to sit up.

She mewed in protest, since that was the only sound she could make. Then watched wide eyed as he stood, walked to the kitchen, grabbed the bottle of champagne, and took a pull like it was a bottle of beer.

His dick stood to attention in his boxers like a flagpole as he knelt in front of her and lifted the bottle to her lips, tilting it only enough so she got a sip and not a shower. Then he took her hand and placed it between her legs, rubbing with his finger over her finger.

She didn't argue, because what the hell was there to argue about?

She touched herself even as he removed his hand and set the bottle back down. She slid her fingers lower to touch inside herself as he rummaged through the pile of clothes, finally coming up with his jeans. He grabbed his wallet, opened it, and pulled out a condom.

Then he obviously saw what she was still doing to herself, and he growled a feral sound that only made her crave him more.

He sheathed his erection, and, like she weighed nothing, he picked her up. Boxed her in with the wall at her back.

Her breaths came more quickly, and her eyes must've gone wide.

Oh, shit. They were doing this.

"Legs around my waist," he commanded, lifting her up, so they aligned perfectly.

She followed his instructions because… Hell. Yes.

He kept their gazes locked while he slid into her millimeter by millimeter. He didn't go fast. The invasion was slow. Tender. Allowing her to adjust to the bulk of him while the connection between them became unbreakable.

When he was seated fully inside her, he kissed her mouth like she was air, and he was drowning.

"I'm sorry," he said. The cords of his neck taut, and the vein along his throat pulsing visibly.

"For what?" she asked. It came out like a whisper because she was well and truly pinned against the wall and she had little air to work with.

"For not sucking your tits against the wall," he said. And then any control he had snapped. He was as feral as the growl before, pumping inside her. Using the wall as leverage to move in and out.

She was not as quiet as she would've hoped, because this was like nothing she'd experienced in her entire life.

"You can come now," he said, as he thrust inside her one more time.

Fully seated there, she tensed around the hard length of him. Her legs held tight around his waist as fresh waves of pleasure pulsed through her.

He finally urged her to put one leg down, and then the other. She used the wall to help hold herself up as he pulled himself from her body. But he didn't have her stay there. He picked her up and carried her to the sofa like she was precious.

Then he covered her with a blanket, dealt with the protection, and finally sat beside her. He pulled her against him and murmured how much he enjoyed what they'd done. Honestly, his aftercare was on point.

"Mach?" she asked his name. "Can I ask a question?"

"Anything."

She reached to trace the scar at his bottom lip. "Where did you get this?"

"Fell off my skateboard when I was twelve and hit my chin on one of those metal railings. It wasn't a big deal." He pressed a kiss to her fingertips. Then he paused, seemingly ready to offer her more. "I, uh, was between families so I was in a group home. Those were the worst, you know?"

She didn't, but her heart hurt for him all the same.

"Who cleaned you up?" she asked, still staring at the scar.

He looked at her funny. "I did."

"Mouth wounds bleed a ton." There had to be blood everywhere.

"Tell me about it. But now I have you, my own personal nurse." He kissed her temple and wrapped his arms around her. "Can't wait to hear what you wanna try after dinner."

She laughed and settled against him, both covered with a blanket. This was pure happiness, wasn't it? And proof that even if this relationship wasn't permanent, it was real.

Chapter Nineteen
DARLA

THEY DIDN'T END up back in bed because they wound up in a limo that dropped them off at Pew, where the rest of Dimefront met up with them. Pew was one of the fancier nightclubs celebrities frequented in Los Angeles. The music pulsed and lights flashed against the walls and ceilings.

There was an entire wall of lights along one side of the room, and an LED dance floor smack in the middle. The walls were all painted matte black throughout the whole club, and the DJ booth stood high above everyone. At one side of the room were two private VIP sections with velvet-lined booths.

One whole section was reserved for Dimefront. The space was separated from the rest of the club by velvet ropes and guarded by burly bouncers who seemed very much into their jobs given the way they glowered at anyone who came close.

Darla started to itch all over because she was more out of place than pineapple on pizza. This was not a good idea.

No, she didn't belong here.

"Darla!" Irina called, then she waved and made a scene, so the other ladies all turned that way, too.

Darla waved back because, well, she couldn't not.

"You good?" Mach asked, eyeing the ladies, then Darla. "Your entourage is calling you."

She nodded. "Totally. I do this all the time."

"You're a natural." He smirked.

"'Cause I can spend money, huh?" she asked, looking up at him and wishing she'd had something cuter to wear than the little black dress she'd tossed in her suitcase, and a pair of flat dress shoes she'd grabbed at Target who knew how long ago. She'd pulled her hair into a high ponytail, added a little blush, and called it good.

But looking at the other ladies? They had gone all *out*. Hair and makeup, tight sparkly dresses, and heels so high they probably needed an escalator to get in them.

Still, Mach looked at her like she was the only woman in the room. That was nice. Really nice.

Darla sauntered over to Irina and the ladies, while Mach did some kind of guy-handshake with Tanner and grabbed a beer from one of the servers.

The waitstaff served up complimentary signature cocktails with names like A-List Affair and Sunset Serenade. Darla went with the Pink Paparazzi because it seemed appropriate given their situation and it came with edible glitter floating in the booze.

The ladies were all there—Irina, Courtney, Becca, and Sam—situated on velvet couches surrounding a small glass-topped table filled with drinks and a few empties that hadn't been pulled yet.

"I'm a little jealous about the *Lately, Later* show invite," Irina said with a fake pout. "It took me ages to nail an invitation."

"You should do it for me," Darla said, cautiously taking a sip of the drink. Holy goodness, it was delish with hints of a pink Starburst candy.

"Oh, no, you definitely get to have this experience," Irina said, like Darla had actually done something to earn it.

Darla shook her head. "I'm good. Promise. You are welcome to do it for me."

"You'll do great," Courtney assured. "The whole thing is practically kindergarten simple. Show up. You be you. Everyone will love you. A little pre-scheduled banter and Mach takes over. He'll redirect the attention to Dimefront and their upcoming album. Ba-da-bing. Done. You go back to your regularly scheduled life."

Well, when put like that it did sound simple. But also, the part about going back to her life felt like it didn't fit anymore.

"What if I fall on my face?" Darla asked.

"Maybe let's not plan on that?" Courtney suggested over the rim of her martini glass.

"I don't think you are giving me the credit I deserve," Darla said. "I can be seriously klutzy."

As if to punctuate the point, she caught a glimpse of the famous Dr. Stone in the other VIP section. He glanced over the room and his eyes caught hers and, honest as all hell, there were not many things that would've made her choke on her Pink Paparazzi, but Dr. Stone winking at her from over in the other VIP section made the vodka just hit differently. She choked, totally choked.

"Don't worry, you get used to it," Sam said, patting Darla on the back to help the vodka go down more smoothly. "They mix 'em strong. Go slow and you'll be fine."

"That's not true," Becca added, holding up a green

concoction. "I've never gotten used to this no matter how slow I drink it."

"No." Darla shook her head. "It's not the drink. I just saw someone, that's all—"

"Who." Irina leaned in like this was intel she had to have.

"It's no one," Darla assured. "I think I got starstruck and was staring a little too hard. Nobody look, it's fine."

All four of the other ladies turned in unison.

"It's either Val or Dr. Stone," Courtney announced, way louder than necessary.

Darla sucked in a breath. Her eyes got wide. "Don't say it so loud."

"You know him?" Irina asked, turning her whole body that direction.

"Not personally." Darla's eyes still felt too wide. "I mean, he's just… he's Dr. Stone. And I know who he is and he caught me staring and then he winked. I choked. That's all."

"Your cheeks are as red as some of the Tens when they get to the front of the VIP line," Irina said with a laugh.

"No." Darla shook her head, trying to be composed. "It's nothing. They're red because the drink went down funny."

"What'd I miss?" Mach asked, his hand resting on Darla's shoulder like he was making sure everyone knew she was with him.

Irina was mid-sip of her drink when she stopped. "Darrrr-lahhh has something to tell you."

Darla covered her lips with her hand. "It's nothing. I have nothing to tell anyone."

Mach held her stare, not even blinking.

"Fine. Yes." She pursed her lips and shot a glare at him.

"I was surprised to see Dr. Stone because I'm a nurse, he is a doctor, and I watch his show."

"She's got a crush." Knox pointed to Darla and bounced on his feet. "She's got a crush. I can tell."

"Stop." Darla rolled her eyes and squeezed Mach's hand. "It's nothing. I'm just…he's just…"

"You are a Dr. Stone groupie?" Mach asked, a hint of teasing and a whole lot of disbelieving. "Never would've guessed that. I thought you didn't do celebrities?"

She stared at him for a beat, because clearly that was not the case.

"Right, well…until…" He gestured to himself.

"I'm not *doing* him." She tossed back more of the Starburst flavored vodka drink. "I *used* to have a crush on him. I still respect what he does. But I am no longer infatuated by his credentials. I have matured in my celebrity desires."

"How 'used to' were you infatuated by his credentials?" Knox asked, as though that was the pertinent part of what she'd said.

"At least a whole week ago," Darla said, joking, mechanically. "And we all know how much can happen in a week, don't we?"

She waggled her eyebrows at Mach.

He gave her a half-grin that was everything.

"What do they call this dude's groupies? If we have Tens, does he have Stoners?" Linx mused.

"Ha." Darla glanced up to Mach to ensure he understood that Dr. Stone was nothing to her. That's why they could all tease about it.

If he meant something, then they sure as hell wouldn't laugh about it.

"You know you can do better than him, right?" Mach asked, a sly twinkle in his eye.

She looked him over from top to bottom, her perusal intentionally obvious. "I definitely do know that."

Chapter Twenty
MACH

WAS THIS REALITY? Because it felt like a dream. A dream that kept going and had him believing his life might actually be changing. It'd only been a week, not long at all. But the way he felt about Darla was different. They had fun, they had sex, they lived without worry—no responsibilities, no stress, just them.

Since Darla arrived in his life, everything had gotten brighter. Almost too bright. The quiet was quieter, the loud was louder.

She was life amplified, and he'd stopped being scared of that and worried it'd disappear. Darla was reality and she wasn't going anywhere.

Except, maybe she was? *Lately, Later* got bumped up to tomorrow and then things would change. He would have to work long hours in the studio with the guys and she'd be going back to her quiet life in Denver, saving lives.

Darla emerged from the bedroom they'd been sharing at Courtney's old place and tucked her cell in her purse.

"Done?" he asked.

"Yup, all good and I gave the green light." She nodded

as she spoke since she seemed to have gotten used to being tabloid fodder. "Courtney thinks this will actually help things along. Feed the beast a little more dinner." She laughed a light laugh.

Not that they hadn't been feeding the media machine for all these days with their impromptu outings—they totally had.

Today was simply the day that Darla fielded calls from national news outlets. All because she'd told a rock star she wasn't interested. And then they ended up on this adventure together, anyway. Apparently, one of the national news outlets planned to run a touchy-feely piece at the end of their broadcast about Mach and Darla and their whirlwind experience after they swiped right on Nocturnal Cupid. The focus was going to be on Darla watching from the sidelines as Mach played with Strummer on the corner of Hollywood Boulevard.

He and the guys had to hit the studio later to prep for *Lately, Later* and try out a few new songs for the upcoming album, so Courtney and Irina were taking Darla out to have a little fun.

"What are you and the girls up to today?" Mach asked, lounging on the sofa waiting for her to finish up with the inventory of her purse before they took off. She did this every time she left the apartment because she might be willing to "roll with whatever" but she'd only do it if she had breath mints and her license.

"We have zero plans except to have an amazing time," she said with a smile as she sauntered to him. She straddled his legs and kissed him like she owned his mouth. He let her and things heated beyond normal living room levels.

"Your mouth is misbehaving," he said, already pulling her T-shirt from the waistband of her jeans, reaching underneath, and yanking one of the cups of her bra down so he had better access to her breast.

He traced his finger over her nipple until she gasped.

"We have to go soon," she said, but she leaned into his palm and then her mouth was on his again.

"We don't *have* to go," he said against her mouth, because there was always the choice to stay home and spend the day inside her.

She rubbed her core against his already hard dick, practically riding him until they were both turned on, even though there were layers of clothes between them.

Fuck, he was either going to get a rug burn from the friction or he was going to come.

The frenzy of their spark was poised and ready to take over.

"I'll be quick," she said, her hand already underneath them to undo the buckle of his pants.

"Gorgeous," he said as he trailed his finger along her jaw. Then he lifted his hips and helped pull off his jeans because there was no way in hell he'd tell her no. She got them down to his thighs and then dropped to her knees. She grabbed the shaft of his erection, and pulled it through the fly of his boxers like it was her own personal lollipop and she was starving for a treat.

Except he was the one getting the treat as she ran her tongue up his shaft and covered the head with her mouth. She traced her tongue along the ridge at the front in the sensitive place that drove him wild. He groaned, dropped his hands to her hair.

She gave him everything, and figured out all the small things that made him crazy and drove him wild. He rode her mouth, and this was bliss.

He wanted to tell her this was so much more than her sucking him off. She'd started to crack the cement walls around his heart, and in those moments when he started to freak the fuck out, she was there to remind him everything would be fine.

But all he said was, "Gorgeous."

It's what he'd started calling her because it's what she was. She seemed to smile against his erection and then hurried things along—holding on with one hand and tucking her fingers under his balls into the spot that always made him come.

Didn't fail this time either, and she latched onto him as he finished, taking it all and swallowing it down.

I love this woman.

Now that thought made him still. He may have just fallen from oblivion, but thinking like that scared the shit out of him.

She pressed a kiss to the tip of his dick and slid up to kiss the edge of his jaw, then his cheek, and then his mouth.

"Gorgeous," he said, holding her gaze with his. "You're amazing."

She smiled, and teased, "The things I can do with my tongue, right?"

But he pulled her to his chest and held on because it was so much more than that and he couldn't put into words because he didn't know any that would do her justice.

So he held her and hoped that was enough. How had she become his everything in such a short period of time? And what was he supposed to do about it?

Since he didn't know how to put it into words, he went down on her until she came twice. And by that point they were both late, but neither of them cared.

He did show up to the recording session with a six-pack of ginger ale in hand to make up for being late.

Mach passed through the room with a huge console filled with countless knobs and buttons that lit up in an array of colors. The tall, white-washed walls of the studio itself were lined with instruments—acoustic and electric guitars, a keyboard, and an enormous grand piano—all waiting to be put to use. The hardwood floors were polished to a shine and the couches were comfortable enough for everyone to take a break when they needed one.

Mach always paused at that moment because he couldn't reconcile the life he knew with this one. That he actually got to live a life where he played in spaces like this was wild.

He had shown up right after Knox. Tanner was already there, setting up shop behind a drum kit, as Linx plugged in his guitar. Bax stared at some sheet music, mouthing the words as he followed the lines, and then singing a few bars in a low tone.

"We havin' a party?" Mach asked, pulling the top off a bottle and taking a slug. "Or are we making some music?"

"Making music," Bax said, glancing up from the music. "After we dissect your current romantic entanglement."

Mach leveled a stare at Bax. "Seriously?"

Linx scratched at his ear and then read from his smart-watch. "We get that this is all new for you, so we are here to support you and help with ideas since we have all been through this part."

"Unnecessary," Mach heard himself say. He would not grin at that or think it was nice that they wanted to help him out. Because he was already in too deep, and he didn't know how to extract himself from Darla at this point if he needed to.

Nobody said anything, but Tanner hit a beat on the drums for one of the new songs they'd planned for the next album. Thank hell for Tanner, who understood Mach did not want to talk this out.

Mach took Tanner's nudge and grabbed his guitar. The other guys fell into line and the music flowed. Bax had written this song about his kid. Another song about how fucking happy he was all the fucking time because he had the motherfucking fairy tale.

The words stuck in Mach's throat, and he couldn't do it, couldn't keep going. Not with Darla all up in his head and the feel of her lips still there on his dick. He swallowed, and he set the guitar on the stand. The guys watched him while they kept playing, but he was out.

He sat on one of the stools off to the side and shook his head.

The music died, and he didn't look up as there was shuffling and the standard sounds of instruments being unplugged and set aside.

"We get it, man." Bax put a hand on Mach's shoulder and said, "We've all been right here."

"I'm being stupid," Mach said, his shoulders tight again. He ran his fingers through his hair, frustration mounting as he tried to make sense of what his life was versus what he figured he deserved.

He blinked heavy as nobody said a word. It started to feel like hours had passed because nobody breathed a syllable.

"No one has anything to say?" he asked, since he figured that's what they'd be doing. Talking shit out like they always did.

"I can't exactly argue with what you said," Linx said, cautiously, almost hesitant. "You are probably bein' stupid."

"You just called me stupid?" Mach asked, because that was not a Linx thing to do.

"You called yourself stupid," Linx pointed out. "We don't know what's up in the land of Mach, so we have to wait until you're ready to tell us. Then we'll decide if your intellectual capacities are still intact." He grinned. "Or not."

"Darla's in my head," he said. And now he knew the sound she made when she came and the sounds she made when she woke up and the little words she whispered while she slept. There was no coming back from that. It branded her as his, and that wasn't fair at all.

"She deserves someone who can be all in," Mach said, resigned to the fact that no matter how badly he wanted to be, he wasn't that guy.

"Why isn't that you?" Tanner asked.

"Shit doesn't last for me," Mach said. "You know that. You've seen it."

"Uh…" Tanner glanced around the room locking eyes with the other guys. "Maybe that was how it used to be for you, but looks to me like your luck changed around the time Linx got pissed at these guys and then we got a shot at playing with 'em."

"And what happens when the band is done?" Mach asked, hating that he voiced the things in his head that he didn't want to hear.

"Yeah, you're bein' stupid." Linx crossed his arms.

"First of all, what the hell?" Bax asked. "Dimefront didn't bring you on as a pity fuck. We don't do that. We brought you on because you're good and you fit, and we like you, and Mach, man, you are family. If we can't make music, then we'll open a fuckin' bakery or something and bake fuckin' cookies together. So wipe the rest of that shit out of your brain. If Dimefront the band dissolved tomorrow, you'd still be our family."

Mach didn't buy it. If Dimefront dissolved, the ties that bound them would, too. That's how it worked.

Mach once had a shot at a family. Nice people, with brothers and everything—the works. He stayed there for a solid six months. Then the dad's job got moved, and they hadn't even started the adoption process. He was still in foster care, and they couldn't take him to another state, so they had to move on and he got bounced to another house.

"What do you think happens to a kid like that when he gets a shot at everything and then loses it?" Tanner asked everyone, glancing around the room to make some kind of point. "They quit reaching for it."

"Not wanting something new is easier than having it and losing it," Mach said. "That's why I'm not it for Darla. I'm not willing to take the risk again. She deserves somebody who is."

"I get it better than anyone," Tanner said, leaning forward so his lanky forearms draped over his knees. "Where we come from? It's hard to believe the good shit is actually meant for us. But, man, you've eaten the shit and now it's time to enjoy that you don't have to anymore."

"Listen to the kid," Bax said. "He's smarter than he looks."

This was great that Tanner thought so, but Mach still didn't buy it.

"Have you and Darla made it official?" Tanner asked in that earnest way of his that made everybody love him. "Put a label on this thing between you?"

What was official anyway? They were together all the time, and they clearly enjoyed each other. But were they official?

"No idea if we are," Mach said, tapping his foot and then forcing it to stop by putting his hand on his knee.

"That's the first thing to clarify," Tanner chimed in. "See where she's at."

"Let's assume we are?" Mach said when nobody said anything else. "We're all labeled up."

"Mach," Tanner said carefully.

"You deserve her and you're falling for her," Knox said. "It's okay. She's a good one. Just don't let it freak you out."

"How do you know that? That she's a good one?" Mach asked, because he knew that—he'd spent countless hours with her already. But they hadn't.

"Courtney thinks she's great," Bax said. "And she requires that I listen to her."

Knox lifted a shoulder. "Anyone who has your undies tied up like this is a good thing for you."

"My undies are not—"

"Hans had her checked out," Linx interrupted. "We know she's legit because, you know, before the big date, he made sure she wasn't a serial killer or anything. Turns out she's actually pretty awesome. Patients and docs love her, solid friends, and a family as average as it gets. So yeah, she's good to go."

That was great. Really. Except—

"Even if I wanted to, I don't even know how to fall in love," Mach admitted. He didn't. He knew family because of what Dimefront, Tanner, and Dan gave him. But he also understood that it was all contingent on other things.

Dan's place to live depended on Mach keeping his nose clean and staying out of trouble.

Tanner was only there for him because he had no other place to be, and they bonded over that. But, eventually, Tanner would have his own family and he wouldn't need Mach anymore.

And Dimefront? They could say all day long that they would always be there. But sure as shit, he knew the band was only there as long as circumstances allowed and fans bought tickets.

"Falling in love is easy," Tanner said. "You just let it happen."

"Sounds like a song you need to write," Mach said. That's the stuff fans loved to hear. All lip service, but they still ate it up.

"You come from a place where we did and you wonder if you're enough for her. I know how that feels," Tanner said. "But you can't let the shit of the past fuck with the goodness of the future."

Tanner did get it. Though his parents were still kicking, so he didn't have the same opportunity for adoption that Mach always fucked up.

"Falling in love is easy. It's like pissing in a twenty-five mile-per-hour wind with a full bladder," Knox announced. "It's a strange relief with a shit ton of frustration."

The other guys nodded along as he spoke.

"And in the end, you feel better about life," Bax said. "'Cause at least you don't have to pee anymore."

"This is the strangest conversation I've ever heard." Tanner scratched at his temple with a drumstick. "But also, not wrong."

"There was this Ten one time. Boston." Linx held up his hands. "That was in the pre-Becca days." He pointed to Bax. "I'm allowed to talk about it. She said so." He seemed to get lost in a memory that Mach was certain he didn't want details on. "She gave head one time with a peppermint candy in her mouth." He shivered. "Weird, and great, and frustrating all at the same time." He pulled his lips to the side. "You kind of hope you never have to do it again, but you don't regret it, either."

"Falling in love is definitely like that." Bax nodded, with a knowing grin.

"Listen, dude, if she's not feeling it, just rely on your good looks instead of your charm," Linx said with a huge grin and a twinkle in his eye.

"I don't want to fall in love with her," Mach confessed with a tinge of uncertainty in his voice.

"It's not something you get to choose." Tanner stared at the wood panels that made up the recording studio floor. "Not something you get to control."

"You know, I think I said something like this before," Knox scowled. "With the wind thing."

It couldn't be that. Because Mach didn't get that.

"Maybe it's just hooking up with a hot girl," he said tentatively, trying on the words for size. But they fit funny—too tight and entirely too wrong.

"If that was the case, we would be playing music right now." Knox blinked. Oh-so-innocent, he blinked.

Bax elbowed Knox in the ribs. "Seriously, man?"

"I'm saying." Knox rubbed at his side where Bax had whacked him. "If he's this tied up, then he should accept that he likes being with her and this is more than just a bang, clang, did my thing."

"And if I admit that I like her? That I think she is literally the one?" Mach asked, trying those words on for size, too. They fit. Felt right.

"Then we can play some music and call it a day," Knox said, tapping out a rhythm on his knees.

"Are you admitting it?" Tanner asked.

"Fucking hell," Mach muttered under his breath, a mix of nerves and relief all through him. He nodded, meeting their gazes with determination. "Yes."

Chapter Twenty-One
DARLA

DARLA WAS in a state of disbelief because she had made it. Her Frontline acceptance landed in her email shortly after Mach left to head to the studio and right before Irina and Courtney came over to pick her up.

> Dear Ms. Davis,
>
> Congratulations! We are pleased to inform you that you have been accepted as a member of Nurses on the Frontline. You will be joining a team of dedicated individuals who are driven to provide quality healthcare to those in need across the globe. …

Frontline even gave her a choice—two off-the-beaten-path clinics in places so remote that she'd definitely have to trek through rough terrain to get to them. They were so far removed from the hustle-and-bustle of her everyday life; it would almost be like starting over on a whole new planet with all new people.

Precisely what she'd wanted when she applied.

This was the part where she was supposed to be excited.

She knew what came next, and that was a good thing.

But she wasn't excited because she realized as soon as she got her acceptance that she'd been crossing her fingers that they would tell her no.

She hadn't even realized it, but that's how it went. She didn't want to be so far away from Mach. Which was silly, because they hadn't even talked about what came next and Mach wasn't the kind of guy who wanted a permanent, or even semi-permanent, woman in his life. He'd made that clear right up front, and she had tried her best to remember that, so her heart didn't get too entangled with promises he didn't make.

"Let's do something fun today?" Irina clapped her hands together with a huge smile plastered on her face. "And not the kind of fun that requires Mach and a motorcycle," she clarified. "I am thinking I make a few calls and we visit my favorite salon over on Beverly Drive and we get the works."

"I could be down with that," Courtney said with a smile, giving Irina a high five.

"I haven't had a spa day... well, ever," Darla mused, already planning what she wanted done. Everyone always talked about how wonderful they were, and what better way to spend the day since there wouldn't be helicopters, illegal motorcycles on a pier, making out on the beach, or ding-dong-ditching Tucker McKay.

"You'll love it," Irina announced. "Nails, hair, the works."

"Like hair *color*?" Darla asked, and a spark of an idea

hit her. Maybe it was because of the time she'd spent with Mach, or maybe it was just *time*, but this kind of change seemed like a good thing.

"Yep," Irina responded as she dialed the salon. "I change mine all the time."

"Quick! Don't think," Darla blurted out to Courtney. "Dark or light?"

"Dark," Courtney answered without missing a beat.

"Pink or purple?" Darla asked.

"For sure purple," Courtney said, seeming to realize there was some decision-making taking place here. "What are we picking out here? Nail color or—"

"Hair color." A huge smile spread over Darla's face. She'd never had the courage to try fun colors in her hair before, but the excitement bubbling insider her made the change too tempting to pass up.

Courtney took a hesitant step back, her eyes narrowing. "Are you sure you want to do this so close to *Lately, Later*?"

"I'll have time to fix it if it's a no go," Darla reassured her, going for nonchalant.

"How?" Courtney asked. "No way you can do that before tomorrow."

"Uh, *Lately, Later* is days away," Darla pointed out. Their adventure wasn't over yet.

Courtney shook her head in clear disbelief. "Mach forgot to tell you, didn't he?"

Darla suppressed a wince because that didn't sound hopeful.

"Tell me what, exactly?" she asked, because he hadn't mentioned anything about *Lately, Later*. Then again, they'd been busy with her tongue down his pants, so… there was that.

"Once more the plan has changed," Courtney announced. "They bumped us up to tomorrow after a cancellation. It's a good thing. Better viewership and a longer time slot. He was, uh, supposed to mention it."

"Tomorrow?" A pit of worry settled in Darla's stomach. In that case, tomorrow marked the start of her reentry into reality, back to being herself, and back to... well, Denver.

"The plan changed. I guess that's what plans do. They develop with time, and we are now evolving with this plan," Courtney said like this was a good thing. "You've got the national news spot. Then tomorrow *Lately, Later*. Everyone is about to be so sick of you two they are definitely going to leave you alone."

"I hate changing plans." Darla pulled her bottom lip under her teeth.

"That's what plans do, though, isn't it?" Irina asked.

Blah, she was right and that was the worst part.

Instead of letting the new timeline wiggle into her head, Darla got purple highlights. Tom would've had a heart attack if she'd done this while they were engaged.

But the highlights looked fabulous. The subtle hint of lavender complimented the ivory of her skin tone and brought out more of the hints of peach in her eyes. She felt beautiful and confident, and it was like the highlights were supposed to be there all along.

Turned out she was a big fan of spa days with Irina and Courtney because her fingernails and toenails matched the same shade of lavender as her hair, so that was kickass.

With her newfound confidence, and their continued encouragement, they picked up those rented Segway scooters she'd reserved on the plane to L.A. And then they made some plans so she could surprise Mach before this crazy journey of theirs had to come to an end. Darla's way of saying goodbye to their adventure, without actually having to say goodbye.

The three of them rolled into the studio on shiny blue two-wheelers while the guys finished up a song she hadn't heard before. Mach was genuinely happy to see her—his face lighting up when he caught a glimpse of her in his periphery. Then his eyebrows raised at the new hair color and his eyes softened and she didn't have to ask if he liked it, because it was written there on his face.

They parked their scooters in the hallway and headed into the studio.

"Hey, uh, Mach?" Darla asked as she meandered to him. She didn't wait before continuing, "Did you forget to tell me something?"

She tap-a-tapped her foot.

He seemed lost at the question.

"Something Courtney maybe asked you to tell me?" She gave him a hint.

"Shit." Mach paled. He pressed his index finger to the bridge of his nose. "Um… *Later, Lately* is tomorrow."

"Uh-huh." Darla nodded, jerking her thumb toward Courtney. "She told me."

"See, Courtney covered it. All good." Linx folded his hands under his chin and looked from Darla to Mach, then back to Darla.

"Anything else I need to know?" Darla asked, smiling a saccharine grin she hoped would distract him from the fact she had an amazing night planned for him.

"No. No," Mach said, adamantly. "And I'm sorry. It skipped my mind when we were, uh, on the couch." He flashed her a knowing smile.

"My couch?" Courtney asked with fake distress. "That's *my* couch!"

"This. Is. Fun." Linx punctuated each word individually.

"Don't worry, Mach." Darla squared her shoulders. "I've forgiven you for your memory lapse. Now, quick, don't think—"

"Black or blue?" Courtney asked, rapid-fire, as she cocked her head and put her hands on her hips.

"Blue," he replied, looking at Darla kind of funny.

"Sweet or savory?" Irina asked.

"Sweet," he said super quick, clearly getting into the game.

"Wool or cotton?" Courtney asked.

"Cotton," he said without hesitation.

"Perfect." Darla raised up on her tiptoes to give him a quick peck on the lips. But when their lips met it was electric, and as he kissed her back it became something more.

Something she couldn't quite put her finger on.

Chapter Twenty-Two
MACH

DARLA'S HAIR wasn't the only thing that had changed today. She was more earnest about their time together. She touched him every second she could, and looked a little sad when he kissed her until she went breathless. Which only made him kiss her until she didn't look sad anymore.

And then, as the sun was setting in the sky over Hollywood, painting the sky in a swirl of blues and peaches, they wound up standing under the Hollywood sign together. The sky was the same color as her eyes, and he was there for it.

"C'mere," she said, pulling him to the side of the W.

He followed and somehow his favorite blue acoustic Fender was laid out on a blanket under the Hollywood sign. A silver bucket with Prosecco sat off to the side, and right next to his guitar was a… black clarinet.

"Blue and sweet were your choices," she said, skip-walking that direction. "The clarinet was mine."

"What is this?" he asked, sliding his gaze to her.

"Well, I know you've been wanting to learn to play the clarinet for a while now, so I thought this would be the perfect opportunity," she said with just the right amount of snark that turned him on and made him want to dominate, all at the same time. "I think you'll really enjoy it."

He stared at her like she'd spent the day drinking the hair dye instead of applying it to her roots.

"I thought we'd make a little music together," she said, nudging him and gripping his hand.

"You arranged this?" he asked, more than a little surprised. A stupid question because, clearly, she had.

"Well, it didn't happen on its own, that's for sure." She moved to the blanket, made him sit with her, and snatched up the clarinet.

"Are you ready?" she asked, ominously.

"I've never been more ready for anything in my life," he replied.

She sat cross legged and, then, defying anything he ever expected, she started sucking on the reed like it was his, well, yeah.

Maybe clarinets weren't so bad after all.

Then she closed her eyes before she sort of played the Stevie Wonder song from the other day on Hollywood Boulevard. It was touch and go, but he was able to work out the melody since she gave it her best shot.

As she played, she opened her eyes wide, like he was supposed to say or do something. But what did a guy do when the girl he was into serenaded him with a clarinet under the Hollywood sign? There wasn't a handbook for this shit.

"I'm not sure how to process this moment," he said, scratching at his neck when she got tangled up in one of the bars.

She lightly punched him in the bicep.

"It's supposed to be a duet," she said with the clarinet still half in her mouth.

"Right." So, that made more sense, for sure.

He lifted the guitar, put the strap over his head, and strummed a few chords. Then she encouraged him with her "sort of" song. Also, he was pretty sure that's what a flamingo sounded like when it got stuck in a swamp and wanted someone to help it out.

He helped her out, playing the notes on the guitar loud enough to drown out the sound of her—well, music was many, many things. He'd just call what she was doing music. Then he sang, and it wasn't Darla on a squeaky clarinet, or Mark Flowers with a new name playing guitar, it was the two of them on a hill in California figuring out how to make the song work despite everything working against them.

They drank some Prosecco, watched the stars, and then headed back down the hill. They got home, and as they always did, they wound up tangled in each other.

Darla's musical talents were iffy, but she was flexible, and that came in handy for all the ways he wanted to take her. Like that moment, with her legs draped over his shoulders, her knees pressed to her own collarbone, and him buried inside of her.

There was a path of their clothing from the front door to the bed. Socks and pants, shirts and underwear leading right where they'd fallen together on the mattress. He'd made the bed before they left earlier, so they wound up on top of the comforter. Naked and breathing heavy while their bodies tangled together.

She moaned as he moved rhythmically, her head falling to the side.

"Eyes," he said with a grunt.

Her twitch of a grin made him even harder. *As if that was possible.* She gave him what he asked for, meeting his gaze full force. Then she trailed her fingertips over his chest, up to pinch his nipples with just enough force to make his dick jump.

He looked up at the ceiling, savoring the feeling.

This was his favorite of all the positions they'd tried, and they'd pretty much tried them all.

While Darla might like the wall best, and he was down with that—because *Darla*—he loved looking in her blue eyes and taking her deep when they were like this. Forehead to forehead, eye to eye, connected in every way.

"Gorgeous," he said as he thrust harder. She made a soft, cute-as-fuck mewling noise he couldn't get enough of.

"I'm close," she whispered, and he could feel the beginning of her orgasm along the length of his shaft. It nearly pushed him over the edge early, but he caught himself and held onto his own release. He'd hold off until she made the one noise right before bliss. He couldn't put his finger on the sound, and definitely couldn't replicate it if he tried. Something like a moan with an undertone of breathy goodness.

Then she made the sound he'd been waiting for—the one right before she finished.

"There it is," he said, adjusting his position so he'd press her sensitive spot more squarely as she clamped around him and held on through the waves.

That was his cue, and as her body pulsed around him, he followed her over the edge.

"Mach," she said his name like it was a prayer, her arms holding him tight against her.

"I'm here, Gorgeous," he said as she continued pulsing around his shaft.

She was trembling and shaking with the force of her release.

"I've got you," he continued to murmur to her.

When they both came back down and he was helping

disentangle her legs from his shoulders, he felt like he was totally bare. His soul, his body… every single part of him.

This was the time he should tell her everything. This was the moment he'd been waiting for—the one where he could tell her he was falling in love, and he didn't know what to do with that. Where he could tell her he'd never learned how to love, so he worried he'd be shit at it, but he was willing to give it a try if it was with her.

She brushed his hair from his face, he hadn't slicked it back after his shower. No need, since it was just the two of them in the apartment and one of her favorite things when they were connected was grabbing his hair. Holding on while they both found release.

One of his favorite things, too, actually.

"Eyes?" she asked, smirking, and thankfully pulling him out of his own damn head.

"Really, Mr. Caveman?" she asked. "You demand my *eyes* in the middle of sex?"

Yes, really.

"This mouth," he said on a growl, leaning into her space with a self-assurance that usually had her dropping all of her guards.

"What about this mouth?" she asked, not giving him an inch.

"I'm really learning to enjoy it," he said with a low chuckle.

"It's almost tomorrow," she said, and her throat worked as she swallowed.

He nodded because, yeah, it was.

Their eyes locked together, and he couldn't say why he decided that was the moment to serenade her, but like all the things with Darla, it just felt right. There in the bed, holding her close, he sang a little of the new Dimefront song he'd co-written about getting it right. He sang to her what he hoped she understood was a promise. He couldn't find the words outside of the bedroom, but he could give them to her here.

Her lips parted and she gasped as he continued singing to her—letting the moment be what it was meant to be.

"That's beautiful," she said when he finished.

He kissed her on the nose, and dealt with the things that needed dealing with while she sat up to grab her shirt.

His throat got thick because he needed to tell her how he was feeling about shit. Explain how fucked up and scared he was about what came next. But when he thought about how to say it, his stomach churned like he'd swallowed gravel and he wanted to puke, but he knew that would only hurt worse.

He'd tell her. He would.

If she could find the courage to play the clarinet for him, he could figure out how to tell her how he felt.

Chapter Twenty-Three
DARLA

THIS WAS the part that had the potential to suck the most. But Darla resolved to make it fun. They weren't done yet, so she lifted her gaze to where Mach brooded on his side of the bench seat in the back of the stretch limo, taking them to the Burbank studio for *Lately, Later*. Mach of a few days ago would've had her on her knees by now. Probably with her top off.

Mach of today was distracted. He stared at his knees, eyebrows furrowed. He'd been that way all day.

There were often patients who came into the emergency department in a place inside their head like this. Often, it was because of some visible medical emergency. But sometimes the culprit wasn't so clear.

She understood where he was coming from—this marked the beginning of the end. But as with everything so far, they had a choice to embrace it while it lasted or… not. In either case, it'd help if he opened up to her so they could figure things out. And it was the only reason her tongue itched to poke and prod so she could get to the meat of Mach's issue. Then they could address it appropriately, and he'd feel better.

As they pulled up to the studio, her nerves tried to kick into gear. She refused to give them any attention, but they were persistent little suckers. The building was tall and imposing. Her breath caught in her throat with the sense of the finality of tonight. The buzz of excitement in the air was infectious, though, and she wanted to be part of that.

"Do you want a mint?" she asked, rummaging through her purse. "I should have one, but I can't find them."

Not that the viewers at home could smell her minty fresh breath, but it was another mini confidence boost to get her through this night.

Courtney had provided a few options for wardrobe, and Darla went with simple. Just a pair of jeans with a purple flowy blouse and stilettos, because Courtney said everyone in Hollywood wore stilettos. She totally nixed Darla's black flats from Target.

Mach placed his hand on her wrist and she breathed a sigh of relief with his touch. Something had switched inside him, and he seemed more like himself.

"You're going to do great," he assured. "I'll be there. I'll make sure."

What happened next was a blur of busy hands directing her where to go. They followed a long hallway lined with framed posters of past show guests until finally arriving at their dressing room. Voices were in her ear, telling her what to do. Makeup brushes on her face, making her look the part.

She'd rather run a trauma bay in the emergency room. It held the same frantic energy, but she understood what was happening there and her role in it a whole lot better.

That was not the case here. This was a tidal wave of activity, and she was body-surfing through it.

Mach got called away since Dimefront would be performing before he went on with her. Courtney stopped by to ensure Darla was good. But this was Courtney's show to run, so she couldn't stay long after Darla assured her she was fine.

And then she was at the set. Darla waited to the side in the shadows until it was her turn. There were studio lights shining on the set and huge cameras on wheels moved all along in the front of the audience. The high ceiling stretched into an abyss above them. Two bulky cameramen stood at the ready in front of several bright lights, while a couple of sound technicians were busy running cables across the room from various pieces of equipment to massive speakers in each corner. A group of producers huddled around a computer monitor discussing something quietly amongst themselves before eventually turning their attention to the stage. And then, they were live.

The teleprompters weren't for her, but boy, wouldn't that have been nice? Unfortunately, they were for Jimmy Jones, the comedian and host of the show. He did his monologue and, yeah, it was funny. Then the Dimefront guys played when they came back from the commercial.

This was a new song. The song Mach had sung to her the night before in bed. She hadn't entirely been paying attention to the words at that point but now that she got a front row seat to their set, the lyrics settled in. They were beautiful words about life and getting it right… everything she needed to hear.

God, this felt like a goodbye song. She'd look forward to hearing it in shopping malls and on social media reels later this year when they officially released it. But right now, it felt like it was just for her. That's the only reason she started to hyperventilate a little.

"Breathe," Courtney said beside her. When had she

shown up? Jimmy did a bit with Bax about Dimefront, their next album, and plans for an upcoming tour. And then it was almost her turn. Her palms got sweaty, and the room started to spin a tiny bit.

Then they introduced Mach and... she had her cue.

The cheers and claps echoed through the sound stage as she walked across in front of the Dimefront crew, waving tentatively at the audience.

"The nurse who turned down the rock star," Jimmy said. "Darla Davis, everybody."

Darla had once delivered a baby in the emergency room parking lot, and everyone did great. During those moments everything seemed to be happening at once, but somehow Darla managed to keep her cool and focus on what she needed to do. If she could do that and not run away, she could definitely do this. In her moment of vulnerability, she summoned the strength from within and willed herself to finish what she'd started.

Every step felt like a test of courage as she strode across the stage, climbed up the stairs, and didn't even stumble a little.

Thank God, she made it to the interview chair between Mach and Jimmy without falling on her face.

"Just a matter of weeks and everything's changed, hasn't it?" Jimmy asked, shaking her hand and leaning in for a hug.

Oh, okay then, he was a hugger, she hadn't realized that. Also, hoo boy, he wore way too much cologne. A whole cloud of it wafted around them all.

Don't sneeze. Don't sneeze.

Mach's hand was at her back, his warm presence a reminder that she wasn't doing this alone. He was here with her, and he was used to this.

"Gorgeous," he whispered in her ear and that one word made all the little hairs stand up along her neck.

Their gazes caught and Jimmy was right there, and there was an audience of people, and the cameras were live, but it still felt like only the two of them.

She blushed a little. "Hi."

"Hi," he responded with a panty-melting grin.

"A true everyday hero in our midst today," Jimmy said. "Great to meet you."

She nodded in response because this whole thing was overwhelming. The lights were super hot, and she was slightly worried that if she opened her mouth, she'd lose her lunch on his desk.

"You've got this," Mach whispered in her ear, casual like he was just a normal celebrity helping her along in front of the cameras, not a guy who knew exactly what to do to make her body purr.

They all sat, the crowd clapped, and her hand itched to reach for Mach all on its own. He seemed to sense that, and clasped their hands together as they sat.

"So, Darla Davis is here." Jimmy Jones said her name again. That was weird, hearing her name as a first-name-last-name so much. "How are things, Darla?"

Okay, phew, that was scripted. That was what Courtney had prepared her for.

"Well, things are interesting," she said, just as she'd rehearsed.

The audience laughed, which was odd because that wasn't super funny.

"You've been on quite the tour of California," Jimmy said. "How did that all start?"

She and Mach talked and worked off of each other, telling their story of how they came to California, and all the things they'd done. Jimmy had tabloid images for a lot of them that he put on the big screen behind them.

"So what comes next for you two?" Jimmy asked. "More California-style fun? A little bungee jumping?"

"Ha, no," Darla said with a glance to Mach. "You heard all about what's going on with Dimefront, they'll be busy for a while."

"What about you?" Jimmy asked.

What about her? That was the million-dollar question, wasn't it? Well..

"I've been accepted into the Nurses on the Frontline program," she announced. "I figure that's where I'll head off to next. A new adventure, this time to give help where it's most needed."

That announcement sat funny in her chest, like she was trying it on for size and it didn't fit at all.

"Hold up. Nurses on the Frontline is that charity where the nurses go away for years, isn't it?" Mach asked.

She nodded. "To all corners of the world to help people who need us."

Did Mach just say a naughty word under his breath? She was pretty certain he did. Was he allowed to do that on television?

"What does that mean for your time with Dimefront?" Jimmy asked, and they all knew he really meant Dime-front's guitarist.

What did that mean? They'd already decided that before things even got going, so it shouldn't have felt so damn off.

"I mean this kind of thing doesn't last forever"—she gestured between herself and Mach—"but it's wicked fun while it lasts, right? But it's time to get back to my not-so-interesting life."

More not-so-funny laugher.

"Then Mach can move forward with being the amazing person he is, too. And Dimefront can make more fantastic music."

"We do make fantastic music," Mach said. Smooth as silk he slid right back into their conversation. "This tour is gonna be epic."

She decided in that second that, "I guess I am ready… I'm ready for my life back. I am so grateful for all this time with Mach, but I never wanted the fame." That's not what this was about.

Jimmy stared at her for a long, uncomfortable beat.

"Everybody wants the fame," Jimmy said, like it was a punchline.

Mach didn't move, didn't touch her. She needed some reassurance from his touch and she hadn't realized just how much until right that moment.

"We've had an excellent side quest together," Mach added. "But we knew from the get-go that it wasn't a forever kind of thing."

The audience made a collective *aww* sound.

Then Jimmy and Mach bantered back and forth after that. Mach deftly took the baton from her as he promised he'd do.

Finally, thank God, finally, they took a commercial break. Darla barely stood before the chair behind her was pulled away by a stagehand and she was escorted off stage.

He frowned. "Frontline, huh? That's new."

Darla swallowed hard. "It is. Brand new, actually. I'm still getting used to the idea."

"You know, it doesn't have to be over with us," he said, pushing his toe into the ground.

"Mach—"

"I mean it. We can keep going. The little side quest doesn't have to end."

"What would I do, just come with you on tour and be your personal groupie?" She meant it as a joke, but it hit a little too hard.

"I don't think it has to be that—"

"We both knew what this was before we started," she said. And yeah, she cut him off, because they could try to drag this out, but it was a vacation that was ending. Part of the reason a vacation is so amazing is because it has a beginning and an end.

He ran his hand over his hair. "No, yeah, you're right."

Funny, though, she didn't feel like she was right.

"If this goes the way Courtney says, then I'll be back at work in Denver in no time."

"That's what you want?" He tucked his hands in his pockets.

What was she supposed to say? No, she wanted to follow him all over the world just so they could be together?

Even if she loved the life with him, he'd start to resent her because she wouldn't be pulling any weight. That wasn't a way to live.

"I guess it's time to get back to living?" she asked.

"I kind of thought that's what we were doing." Mach pulled his lips into a thin line.

"Life can't be all fun and games, there's a reality out there where we're needed." As much as that stung, it was the truth.

Chapter Twenty-Four
MACH

HE KNEW how it would end before they even got started. So his heart shouldn't have hurt so bad at the revelation that the time was up. There was no snooze button on their relationship. It was done, and that's how Darla clearly wanted it.

They headed back to the apartment quietly, both understanding this was the end point. They'd known when they started there would be an ending, and this was it. But he'd let his heart take the lead, and that was the first mistake.

Darla didn't talk, not even to rehash a little of what had happened on the show. She stared out the window of the limo as Los Angeles passed by outside, her hands folded in her lap and her face expressionless.

But he couldn't do it. He couldn't pretend like this wasn't killing him, so the second they got back he took a shower. Took a breather to get himself back together.

The water rained down on him, washing away the stench of *Lately, Later* and any hope he'd held onto that this might end differently.

Talk about a fucking mess.

He never should've put himself on Nocturnal Cupid. Never should've come up with the stupid contest to win a date with him. Never should've put himself in a position to feel this much for another person.

He'd get a small taste of the goodness of the world, but he never got the whole thing. The key to living was going to have to be avoiding those tastes so he wouldn't know what he was missing.

He finished his shower, dressed, packed his duffel, and found Darla on the sofa like he'd discovered her countless times before.

Ass to ankles on the sofa, staring out the open window.

He hated this part. Of all the parts that came with caring for a person, letting them go was the thing he hated most.

"The Frontline thing's gonna be kickass," he said. "Good for you, making that happen."

She'd applied. She landed it. She should do it.

She glanced away from the window to him, her expression hardening at the sight of the duffel bag. He set it down beside him.

"Why?" she asked.

He wasn't sure if she was asking why about the Frontline situation or about the duffel bag. But either way—

"It's what you want." He lifted a shoulder. "I respect that."

The hard expression etched on her face turned to nothing again. She was unreadable.

Unreadable was better than hurting, so he'd take it.

"What if I change my mind?" she asked quietly, pointedly checking out his duffel. "It's a scary thing to move on from everything you know. You know?"

He knew better than he'd ever tell her.

"If you don't want to go save lives where they need you most, then you should find what you do want. Chase after that with everything you've got." He crossed his arms, leaned against the doorjamb. "You deserve all the good stuff, Gorgeous."

She deserved her dose of happy, and he wanted that for her.

"I don't want to be stuck again. And I don't want to be on influencer feeds, and I sure as hell never want to do *Lately, Later* ever again in stilettos," she said, adamantly.

"That's a lot of things you don't want," he agreed.

"I want more than all of that."

"What do you want, Darla?" he asked, already regretting the question as soon as it left his mouth.

"What if I can't have what I want?" she asked, blinking away wet tears so quick it was like they never even happened.

He'd never forgive himself for making the crack that formed in her impressive facade. He nearly broke and gave in to what he wanted. To tell her all the things about him and beg her not to go anywhere.

But this was the stopping point, and if they dragged it out, it'd only hurt worse. If he held on that long then the end would be unbearable. He didn't think he could get through that.

"I don't get to keep you, Gorgeous," he said, instead of explaining any of it. Explaining how, for him, all the good things never lasted. So he held on while it made sense and then let go when the time came. He'd gotten great at it, actually. Things were easier all around this way. "But it's sure been fun while it lasted."

"That's it, then, huh?" she asked, biting at the edge of her bottom lip.

"Yeah," he said, rubbing his hand over his jaw. She

made it clear what she didn't want, and if she stayed with him, that's exactly what she'd get.

So tomorrow she'd go back to Denver, and tonight he had to let her go. Tonight he'd be the one to leave so she didn't have to take that on.

Darla stood from the sofa, strode to him, put her hands on his shoulders. "I'm not ready to say goodbye."

He wanted to laugh and give her that, but he couldn't.

"Darla, this stuff?" He laid his hand on her hip. "It doesn't last. It just doesn't."

"Not if we don't let it." She gripped his shoulders.

Why was she pushing so hard for something that would break him? "Darla, go be happy."

"Don't tell me what to do."

He extracted himself from her grip. "You're right. That's not my place."

"What if I decide I want it to be your place?" she asked, the words fiercely gentle.

Her words were strong, certain. But her expression shifted to erase the little sliver of hope he hadn't realized she still carried until it was gone.

"Maybe I'm finally ready to give it a shot with someone who doesn't need to be fixed." She tossed her hands up. "And *that's* when things end?"

"What do you mean, someone who needs to be fixed?"

"You're not a fixer-upper, Mach. You're the real deal."

That's where she was wrong. So he grabbed his duffel in one hand and pushed her hair behind her ear with the other. "Best to do it now, before we're in too deep."

"Mach." She said his name, tossing it right at him like a blade.

He should tell her and explain, so she would understand. "It's not that I don't want to see this thing with us go further, but it won't last and we need to accept that now so we don't get hurt. I refuse to do that to you."

Her hands went right to his chest and he held them there.

"There's a difference between being unable to do something and being totally unwilling," she said. "Then I guess that's it, huh?"

Why did he feel like he'd been kicked in the gut? He was the one making the call to leave.

He turned. "You deserve everything."

He said nothing, because there was nothing left to say that would help. It'd all been said already.

Chapter Twenty-Five
MACH

IN THE WEEK following the *Lately, Later* appearance, Darla flew back to Denver with Sam. Mach and the guys finished up some work in the studio before they headed back, too. And in the midst of that, one of the more popular A-list heartthrobs found out he had a secret identical twin. A separated-at-birth tabloid story did the trick and, just like that, no one was talking about Darla at all.

Word had it—from Hans—that she was back at the hospital and no one knew if she'd accepted any Frontline assignments. At least, no one told him if she had.

But it was none of Mach's business, anyway.

So things were back to normal. Darla got to go back to her life, and Mach floated on his pizza slice in the pool instead of sorting his shit. His days were spent with the sun warming his skin with a soundtrack of water lapping against the sides of the pool. Weightless and sprawled out on the float, he willed his brain to stop going back to her. The damn thing was on autopilot, though, always thinking straight back to her in a constant torment he couldn't shake.

Which was why his time in the pool did not spark joy anymore. He kept it up because at least it was better than all the alternatives he'd come up with—those being getting drunk at Brek's or actually sorting his shit.

"Time's up," Tanner said, his voice coming from the edge of the pool.

Mach cracked open an eyelid, squinting against the sun. "Huh?"

"Time's. Up," Tanner said, again, this time with more insistence.

Water splashed against the edges of the pizza slice as Mach twisted to see what Tanner was going on about. What the hell was his problem? Tanner was dressed like he always was, he didn't even have trunks on or a towel, so why did he need the pool?

"For what?" Mach asked, sitting up on the float, his legs dangling off the side of the pepperonis.

"For this whole thing." Tanner gestured to the floating pizza slice and the pool. "You're done." Again, he sounded firm, like he knew what he was talking about, but it made no sense at all.

Before Mach could even roll off the plastic into the pool, Dan's voice came through the yard. "Mach, get out of the pool."

Son of a bitch—

"You brought Dan?" Mach asked, both appalled that Tanner would bother Dan like this, bring him all the way out here for nothing. And, also, a little ashamed that Dan would have lots of things to say to Mach about how disappointing his behavior had become.

Dan always had lots of things to say when his boys got up in their own heads. He approached the side of the pool, crossing his arms beside Tanner. "Out, Mach. Time to talk."

He said this in the same tone he'd used when Mach was fifteen and had just landed himself an in-school suspension for the third time that semester. That time he'd found himself in the principal's clink for organizing an unauthorized concert in the school cafeteria where everyone beatboxed to the old-school *I'm Too Sexy* by Right Said Fred, while Mach stood on one of the tables doing hip thrusts and singing the lyrics. The disruption got him suspended, but the legend of the cafeteria concert probably still lived on.

Mach rolled off the slice and swam to the edge of the pool, extracting himself from the water. He may have been an adult who made his own decisions, but he knew Dan would happily pull him off the pool float by his ear if that's what it took.

"You met a girl and it got serious?" Dan asked, hands on his hips and getting straight down to business.

Mach nodded. "Serious is probably an appropriate word."

"You didn't think to tell me about it?" Dan asked, and he wasn't being mean, he was being a dad. All these years later, and that still made Mach feel weird inside. Sort of happy, but also scared, because the other shoe would drop.

"It happened and then it was over. Didn't take long," Mach said, looking everywhere but at the man he called his dad.

Dan was twenty years older than Mach and Tanner, but other than the gray hair he'd earned from being their foster dad, he didn't look it. Dan worked with his hands, so they were perpetually stained no matter how much he scrubbed at them. And the guy could hold a tune—he'd been the one to encourage Mach and Tanner to live their musical dreams.

"You broke it off with her?" Dan asked, handing Mach a towel laid out on the patio furniture.

Mach took it, and wrapped it around his waist, nodding.

"You broke it off with this Darla, who I never got to meet?" Dan was going in circles here.

Clearly, he already knew, since he was there.

"He broke it off because she makes him happy," Tanner accused, filling in an unnecessary blank.

"Why is this happening?" Mach gestured to the circle of them.

"Because we're your family and when you are hurting, family backs you up," Dan said, and the weight of his stare was enough to make Mach look up.

"Can't believe I have to explain this, yet again," Dan whispered, totally exasperated. "But I'll keep explaining it until it sticks."

"I did it for her." Mach pushed his hair back out of his face, using the water to hold it there. "It's what's best for her so she can be happy."

"Did you take idiot pills this morning?" Tanner asked. "Is that what happened?"

Dan stared Tanner down like he needed to shut it. But Tanner didn't shut it.

"She's not happy, man," Tanner said, sliding the knife into the kidneys. "Sam and Courtney, Becca and Irina? They've all been checking in on her. She's getting through her days, doing what she does, but she's not happy."

"She will be," Mach assured. She only needed a little time. "Happier than I can make her."

"You take yourself away from people who care about you," Dan said, matter-of-factly. "It's got to stop because, now, you're hurting people. And, worse yet, you're hurting yourself."

"Because that's what I do. I hurt people." Mach forced his chin not to tremble, but standing here with Dan and Tanner, who had seen him at his worst? He knew they caught the small show of weakness. These guys also understood the destruction Mach left in his wake. "I'm saving her from the hurt."

Eventually, these two would get tired of him, too. But every time he'd tried to scrape them as a kid, they'd held on tighter.

"Hold up." Tanner held his palms up in surrender. "Are we doing this again?"

Dan rubbed his hands together, chewing on something in his mind. Finally, he said, "Family doesn't leave. You aren't getting rid of us."

They hadn't left *yet*.

Mach didn't have to voice the thought because Dan pulled him into a tight hug. He'd done that when Mach was fifteen, but it'd been a long time since then. "Stop feeding yourself shit when you know you deserve lasagna."

Mach couldn't help the laugh; it came out all on its own. That was a Dan-ism if he'd ever heard one.

"I'm not sure what to say to that," Mach said, scratching at his ear because his skin felt too tight.

"Then say nothing," Dan suggested.

"You have a family now and it may not be what normal people get, but since when have we ever been normal?" Tanner asked.

"Found family is the best kind," Dan said, tilting his chin toward the house.

Mach followed his gaze to where all of Dimefront and their girls stood on the grass lined up behind him, watching the show.

"We are the *best* because we choose to love you even

when you're being a dipshit," Knox amended Dan's statement.

A bubble of something grew in Mach's chest. Hope? Was this hope? Or was it just happiness? He wasn't an emotional guy, but maybe it was time to re-evaluate.

He met the band halfway on the path, took a deep breath, and asked, "How do you even get a girl back?"

"Well, first you ask nicely," Knox said, arm slung around Irina.

"Then you buy her something outrageous," Linx added. "I bought Becca a sports car."

"Write her a song," Bax suggested, with Courtney tucked into his side.

"Flowers?" Tanner asked, kissing Sam on the temple. "Maybe hire a skywriter?"

"You are all idiots," Courtney said, crossing her arms even as she snuggled into Bax's side. "Darla doesn't want any of that." She paused, thought about it. "I mean, she probably wants all of that—not the skywriter—but really, what she wants is you, Mach. That's all she wants. She knows it, but she doesn't know how to reach for it either when you've taken yourself so far out of her grasp."

"I don't know how to do this," Mach admitted.

"That's why you have us," Knox said, and the shit-eating grin wasn't totally necessary.

But it was Knox.

This was Dimefront. They were his family, and they had his back.

Chapter Twenty-Six
DARLA

"PUNCTURE WOUND in exam five is ready for discharge," the hospital clerk said, handing Darla the chart.

Darla took it and brushed her bangs out of her face. She needed to get them trimmed soon, and it was probably time to let the purple go. Her nursing supervisor made it clear she didn't like it, even if there wasn't exactly a hospital rule about it.

"I'll handle that before I take off," Darla said. "Dr. Brewer needs to do another panel on exam one." She flipped the pages to check her notes once more. "Numbers are still higher than they should be."

Life was normal.

Life should've been great.

Her throat got thick at the memory of floating pizza slices in the pool and arguing with Mach over how messed up things had become, and then not arguing and going on adventures all over Los Angeles.

That was laughable now, because her life was exceptionally normal. Courtney was right—she'd fed the beast of the media machine, and then it had gone on to greener pastures. And yet, she wasn't happy, because all the normal in the world didn't fill the void Mach left behind.

She missed him so much she couldn't catch her breath sometimes. So she picked up extra shifts at the hospital, hung out with Patrice and Renata, scheduled a trip to visit her family in South Dakota and spend time with her niece.

He left after *Lately, Later* and that was that. She flew back on her own, and kept her nose out of all things Dimefront. Though the other Dimefront women weren't so keen to let her go back to her regularly scheduled life. When they all got back to Denver they insisted on staying in touch. And Tanner, too. That was an odd one because he kept calling, insisted the only way he'd stop bugging her was if she agreed to a meet. This was great and all, but Darla needed to get home. That frozen burrito wouldn't microwave itself. Still, she was headed to Brothers' Garage after work. The *only* reason was to ensure Tanner knew she was alive and living her life, not because she wanted to know how Mach was or what he was doing.

The nurses' station was located near one side of the hallway, allowing them to keep an eye on all rooms from a central location. The hallways were wide enough to fit two gurneys side by side, and windows lined one side of each corridor, letting in light when people were often in their darkest places.

She hustled to exam five with the discharge papers in her grip. Taking a deep breath, she checked the notes. Then before stepping into the room, she did three pumps of hand sanitizer, knocked quickly, and peeked in.

"Ready to go home?" she asked, pulling back the curtain.

A gurney was at the center of the space, with white sheets tucked in tight and a small pillow at the head. On either side of the bed were machines with digital screens that displayed heart rate readings and oxygen levels.

There was no patient in the room, and no puncture wound in sight. Only Mach, sitting in the chair off to the side. Lounging like he was supposed to be there. His hands in the pockets of his jeans, his hair slicked back, and his beard freshly trimmed. The man she'd tried so hard not to fixate on, sitting right there in front of her.

The sight of him was a kick in the stomach and a giant hug she didn't realize she needed, all happening at the same time.

"Are you okay?" Darla asked, scanning the paperwork the clerk had passed her. Bogus paperwork, it seemed.

"I guess that depends on how this goes," he said, and he was a little paler than normal.

"You're not feeling well?" She set down the papers and started toward him to check his vitals.

"I never had stability," Mach said, standing and essentially stopping her forward momentum. "You need to know that. I was a hard kid to love, and I got passed from family to family so much I started to believe it was all my fault. It being everything."

"Mach?" She glanced between him and the rest of the room. None of this made any sense.

"I didn't tell you this stuff because I don't like to think about it," he said before keeping on, "I was one of those foster kids who didn't have it as bad as others." He paused, thought about that. "My story wasn't that bad. Parents passed away. No family. That was just my life. It's all I knew. Until Dan, I never really had someone give a shit, you know?"

Darla shook her head because this was not her place. "Mach, I… I don't know why—"

"I need to tell you," he said through what seemed like a

whole heaping amount of pain. "Will you stick around long enough to hear it?"

He pulled his lips in like he was hoping she'd give him good news and stay.

She'd do anything for him, so she nodded and stayed right where she was. "Okay."

He came closer, but he didn't touch her. He sat on the foot of the gurney and folded his hands in his lap.

"I had a shot at a family once," he said. "It didn't stick, and, uh, knowing you aren't good enough to keep the people you love? That they'll take off? That shit hurts."

She nodded, encouraging him along.

"It's hard to care about a kid when they've got every wall up they could build over all those years," he said. "That's what Dan told me, anyway."

"He cares about you," Darla said on a whisper.

Mach nodded. "I came to him when everyone else counted me out."

"Why are you telling me all of this?" Darla asked. "You made it clear it won't work for us."

"Yeah, I'm sorry about that. I made a mistake because I figured it'd hurt less if we ended it before we got in too deep." He paused, swallowed hard. Gripped and ungripped his hands. "But, Gorgeous, I realized too late that I am already in too deep."

Oh, okay…

"I would like to give us a solid try. If you're willing," he said, his voice strong but his expression gentle. "If you've got to go save the world, then I'll wait. And I'll be right here when you're ready for me."

She would not cry. *Not going to cry. Not going to cry.*

"Because when a guy cares about a girl as much as I do you," he continued, "he's willing to give her everything she wants. If that means waiting, then that's what it means."

He reached into a crumpled brown paper sack she hadn't noticed in his grip and placed a bobblehead that looked a whole lot like her on the table beside the bed. "You deserve everything, Gorgeous. Starting with your own... *you*. And, uh, you know where to find me. Whenever you're ready. There's no rush."

Her gaze was glued to the bobblehead of herself, her mind turning over all he'd said. Her eyes misted and the thick weight of forever without him lifted from her shoulders.

Mach stood and wadded the paper bag in his hand. And then he strode to the door, opened it, and left.

Like, he actually walked out the door.

He rocked her world and then he left.

She hurried to follow him, stopped herself and went back for the doll, then back to tracking him down.

The hallway was mostly empty, and he'd nearly made it to the bank of elevators before she caught him.

"Mach!" she called before he could press the button.

He turned, and his expression went funny as she ran to him. That magnetic pull too much to fight any longer. She didn't give him the chance to do anything but catch her as she tossed her arms around his body and held on.

"Stop walking away," she said against his neck.

He held her close, his hand at the back of her head like she was precious. "Okay. All right."

"I turned down the Nurses on the Frontline placement," she said. That seemed like something he needed to hear.

The relief in his eyes was everything she needed to keep going.

"I'm not going anywhere," she promised, as her feet found the ground once more.

"Why?" he asked, studying her face like he'd forgotten what she looked like.

"Because what I want isn't there," she said, gripping the lapels of his jacket. "It's here. In a swimming pool on a pizza slice."

He grinned a half grin.

"It's you, you lug nut." She went in for another hug, but this time his mouth met hers and even though it was the most unprofessional thing she'd ever done at work, she let him kiss her.

"So we're both willing to give the space, but neither of us wants it?" Mach asked, his thumb tracing her cheekbone.

She snuggled against his chest. "That's what it sounds like."

"We could do the whole get married thing someday, if you want?" he asked like that was an actual proposal.

She pressed her face into his chest. Because this was one of those dreams that she didn't want to compromise on again.

She opened her mouth to tell him she wanted this to be it. And for this to be her everything, she couldn't skip any of the parts that meant something to her. Starting with that special proposal. It was important. She loved him all the same, but could she please have more than just an "if you want"?

What she said wasn't that. "I'm going to require an actual proposal with you on your knees."

"One knee?" He lifted his eyebrows.

She smirked. "I don't know. You do good work when you're on both knees."

That bought her a full belly laugh.

"I love you, Mach," she whispered, pressing up on her toes to press a quick kiss to his mouth.

He wasn't having it. No, this time he took her mouth like he owned it. And when they finally came up for air, they were both breathing hard.

"I love you, Gorgeous. That's never going to change."

Chapter Twenty-Seven
DARLA

DARLA STILL HAD to catch up with Tanner, and Mach agreed to tag along since they weren't going to be spending much time apart for at least the immediate future.

Her hand was tucked in Mach's as they walked through the parking lot at Brothers' Garage. The parking lot was vast and tucked behind a chain link fence with wire at the top. The asphalt was filled with an eclectic mix of vehicles in various stages of repair, everything from vintage Mustangs to newer Toyotas all lining the parking spaces of the lot.

"How did you even get in?" Darla asked, swinging their hands together. "There's loads of security at the ER and they don't let anyone just walk through."

"A little magic from Hans and a whole lot of help from your friends," he said, staring at her like he couldn't believe she was there with him. "Patrice and Renata were extremely helpful."

She owed them, then, didn't she?

He showed her the way to the back garage and through large metal doors marked as *Employees Only*.

"It's cool, I work here sometimes." Mach grinned another of his sly smiles that she'd missed so much.

The smell of gasoline and oil permeated the air in the open garage. Tanner was there talking to another guy—older, clearly a mechanic based on the overalls and the dirt in the creases of his hands. His name tag patch read, *Dan.* They both stared up at a car on a hydraulic lift, pointing at things she wouldn't even try to understand.

Ask her about ventricular reticulation and she was all about it. But with cars? Duct tape and WD-40, always.

Car parts were strewn about under the vehicle they worked on, tools scattered around like forgotten toys. Everywhere there was evidence that multiple projects were underway here. Things being fixed. It felt a lot like the hospital, really.

"Tanner?" she said like a question.

He shifted his gaze to her and the smile he gave was brilliant. "Darl-ahhhh."

His expression lit up even more seeing her holding hands with Mach. Then he gave Mach a head nod that seemed to hold a whole lot more than the simple movement implied.

Dan came out from beneath the car, wiping his hands on a rag. This was Mach's family and what they thought was suddenly important. That's why her hands were shaky. But she had Mach, now, and that's all the courage she needed.

"You're Darla?" Dan asked, giving her a once-over like a parent deciding if a person was good enough for their kid. "I'm Dan."

Darla held her free hand to him. He shook it with a firm handshake she met squeeze for squeeze.

"I am." She bounced on her toes, sort of wishing she'd

taken time to change out of her boxy scrubs. But, then, there wasn't time.

"This is my dad." Tanner draped his arm around Dan. "Mach's dad, too."

Mach nodded and something profound but unspoken passed between the three of them.

"He is," Mach said.

Dan got a little choked up at that declaration. He coughed to cover it up.

"I'm glad you came, Darla." Dan gestured to a cluster of three sofas all pushed together to make a U shape in the corner. Thin blue fabric covered the couches, with a stained beat-up coffee table between them. There were a couple of vending machines right near there, too.

"I just came to tell Tanner that things are fine," she said. "Well, before they were fine. Now they are excellent." She glanced up at Mach. Excellent, indeed.

"You want something to drink?" Dan asked.

"No. Thank you. I'm…uh…" She was what? Ready to go home and microwave a burrito? "Actually, yeah." She didn't have anywhere to be but right there.

"You two worked shit out?" Tanner asked, tossing a Coke to Mach, and then cracking open one for himself.

Mach settled on one of the sofas and tucked Darla right beside him.

"Yup," he said, opening the can and handing it to Darla.

"Tell me about yourself," Dan said, sitting across from them, clearly ready to hear all about her. "This is the first time Mach's ever brought someone for me to meet."

"I'm a nurse, I try to fix people. It's sort of my thing." Darla tucked a stray piece of hair that fell from her ponytail behind her ear. "But I'm not sure what's going to happen now that we're giving this a go. I guess I'll have to figure out how to be Mach's number one groupie and still do what I love."

"You will," Dan said, nodding. "As long as you understand that he's not broken. *He* doesn't need fixing." Dan pulled his lips into a line, sinking into his thoughts. "That's the problem. People always thought he was broken, but he wasn't. The kid doesn't need fixing. He needs to be loved."

Darla's throat got thick. That was profound. Mach squeezed her tighter against his side.

"And if there's a time that he won't let me?" This Darla asked, looking up straight to Mach.

But it was Dan who answered, "Something I learned a long time ago working with these kids—they'll always let you in, if you wait 'em out. That's the trick. You see them as a whole person and eventually they will too." Dan looked at his shoes. "I thought Mach was there already, but I was wrong. I think he is now."

"Mach?" Darla asked.

"I'm there." He lifted his thumb to trace her lip. "I'm there, Gorgeous."

And she believed him, because that's what people did when they loved each other. When they found the perfect matching half that made them realize they were whole the entire time.

Epilogue
MACH

MACH HAD ONE QUESTION, and that question was, "What the fuck?"

He and the guys finished up the last show in Edinburgh and then they took the red-eye home early to surprise the girls. The girls who all came home two weeks ago to, apparently, tear shit up.

"Whoa," Tanner said, stepping beside him.

"What time is it?" Mach asked, not looking to Tanner but lifting his sunglasses and squinting as he kept his eyes on the insanity that was their backyard.

"No idea," Tanner replied. "Maybe this is a dream, and we need to wake up."

That didn't make sense, since the sun was up, and Darla and Sam were in the backyard of the house they all shared. Darla had moved in, and she and Mach had their half of the monstrosity while Tanner and Sam had theirs.

Right now, though, Darla was laughing and pointing at something off to the side while Sam beamed with pride.

That wasn't the part that had him swearing. No, the part that had him swearing was the part where the sidewalk leading from the back door of the house to the pool and then the gate was all torn to shit. There was a construction crew working in a flurry of madness as they poured new cement into molds where the perfectly fine old cement had been when they'd left for Scotland.

"Darla?" he called, heading towards her.

She glanced to him, then waved her hands, shouting, "You're not supposed to be here! Don't look!"

Those were the words she said, but she still ran at him like she always did when they'd been separated for any length of time. She jumped up into his arms with such force he fell back on one boot.

"Seriously, don't look," she said, earnestly.

"That's not the hello I was thinking I'd get," he said, even as she squeezed the stuffing out of him.

"It's not done," she said. "You can't see it yet."

"Gorgeous, I've already seen it." He set her down and took in the scope of a project he had no idea was happening.

"Here's the thing." She patted his chest. "Sam and I had an idea and we thought it'd be fun. But you're not supposed to be home for two more days. So it's still a mess."

"What's the idea?" he asked.

"C'mere," she said, skip-walking to the side of the new path. She pulled back a tarp and there was a pink star in black granite like they'd seen on Hollywood Boulevard. Except this one had his name on it in gold.

He quickly glanced away, overwhelmed with emotion. His throat felt tight and his eyes watered. He had to take a deep breath before he could look back at her. While he'd gotten a little more used to the touchy-feely shit since Darla became a permanent fixture in his life, it hadn't prepared him for this right here.

"Oh," he said.

"I promise, it'll look really great when it's done," she assured. "Irina, Becca, and Courtney are all doing this in their backyards, too. We're connecting them together. It's your own personal Dimefront Walk of Fame."

"You made me a star?" he asked, still a little numb from the realization that she'd done this whole thing.

"No, you made yourself a star," she said, with a small smile. "I'm just planning the ceremony."

"*You* planned all this?" he asked, his heart swelling with pride.

"If you like it? Then... yes," she said, sort of confidently. "If you don't, then it was all Sam's idea."

She was teasing, and he loved it.

He'd had a plan for this part, but the moment felt right and he decided to roll with it.

"Right or left?" he asked.

"Left," she said, jumping right into their game.

"Yes or no?" he asked.

"You know the answer's always yes," she said, her eyes light with laughter.

"Check the left pocket." He gestured to his coat pocket and she reached inside, pulling out the ring box he'd tucked there.

There was another tucked in the right pocket, too. Just in case.

She flipped open the top, and by the time she looked back at him, she had tears in her eyes.

Lucky for him, she'd already said yes. But she said it again anyway, for good measure.

He wrapped her in a fierce embrace because she'd become his family, and they'd never been happier.

"Mach?" she asked, her face squished against his chest.

"Mm hm?"

"You're not down on your knee," she said with a harder squeeze.

"I can't, you're holding on too tight," he said against her hair.

"Good point," she said, squeezing harder. "I like it this way better, anyway."

And just like that, Mach's life was fucking fantastic.

Guess Who's Next?

Zach Dvornakov is finally getting his story told in the final installment of the Mile High Matched series.
Babushka is busy preparing all the details.
Can't Believe You Came is coming Fall of 2023!

Acknowledgments

Okay, well team, we made it.

Are we cutting it so close to the deadline that I feel we might fall off the razor thin edge of sanity remaining? Yes.

Did my ear drum burst as I was wrapping this baby up? Also, yes.

Is it refilling as I type this? Yuppers.

Am I going to sleep for a week after release? Damn straight.

Holly Ingraham, well, yeah.
Girl. You are the definition of an angel.

Thanks, as always, to my family: Steve and all four of our children. Mom, thanks for giving me a writing cave to escape into. Sereneti, thank you for always enjoying my stories and telling me so.
Thanks to those writer friends who keep me grounded: Dylann Crush, Serena Bell, Jody Holford, Brenda St. John Brown, Claire Marti and so many others that I'm spacing right now because… ear drum.
Thank you to Autumn Gantz my publicist and manager. She's the one who keeps things moving with Team Christina.

Thanks to Amanda Wallace who held my hand when I wanted to quit and go work at a donut shop instead of finishing this story.

Thanks to Anna Gorman who helped me figure out how to make Mach's story unique.

Beth Carbutt… welcome to Team Christina. Thank you for working your magic on this manuscript.

Karie you make me so happy. Thank you for being my bestie.

Gretchen… what can I say? Let's pick a writer's retreat hotel that's not haunted next time. Seriously, though, thanks for being here for me.

Gina… I am so grateful we have reconnected after all this time. I'm so blessed to call you my friend.

Thank you to Tara Wine-Queen for alpha reading the first chapters.

Emily Sylvan Kim, agent extraordinare, thank you so much for all you do for me and my books. I just adore you.

Audrey Nelson, thank you for the awesome copy edits! You really came through for me and I am so damn grateful.

Shasta Schafer you are the bomb diggity when it comes to proofreading. Thank you, thank you!

Denise Allen—my friend and supporter—thank you for loving my books and always being there for me.

Thanks to the team at Blue Nose Audio for the fantastic narration and audiobook production.

Thank you to Lindee Robinson Photography for the fabulous photo of Daniel I got to use for this book.

And thank *you*, yes YOU, for making my dream of being an author a reality. This is a pretty great job I've got!

About the Author

Christina Hovland lives her own version of a fairy tale—a retired artisan chocolatier turned romance writer. Born in Colorado, Christina received a degree in journalism from Colorado State University. Before opening her chocolate company, Christina's career spanned from the television newsroom to managing an award-winning public relations firm. She's a recovering overachiever and perfectionist with a love of cupcakes and dinner she doesn't have to cook herself. A 2017 Golden Heart® finalist, she lives in Colorado with her first-boyfriend-turned-husband, four children, the sweetest dogs around, and Mayonnaise the wonder cat.

Emmaline Is Ready!

** Turn the page for chapter one of
It Doesn't Have to Be This Hard! **

From USA Today bestselling author Christina Hovland comes a single parent, #DateMyCelebrityDad, forced proximity romance.

Divorce her Beverly Hills husband: check. Set the neighborhood dumpster on fire with her nightstand buddy… check. Her hunky celebrity chef neighbor rushes to her aid? Sigh. Check mate.

After that introduction Emmaline Eaton is doing her best to avoid the attractive chef, but their daughters just became the bestest of friends.

Ethan Greene's culinary show and career are in shambles. He already has too much on his plate trying to figure out the single parent life when his daughter launches a trending hashtag of #DateMyCelebrityDad. Now he's getting all kinds of unwanted attention, so he calls in a favor from Emmaline. If she could just pretend to be his date until the social media mayhem dies down, that would be fabulous.

But when their kids play matchmaker, just how much heat can Ethan and Emmaline handle?

** Originally on preorder as Everything's Fine, Emmaline*

Chapter One

THIS FIRE? Not her fault.

Well, mostly not her fault.

Fine, a little bit not her fault.

Sonofabitch, it was *totally* her fault.

Her fault for always saying yes. Her fault for marrying the wrong man. Her fault for divorcing him. Her fault for thinking she deserved an orgasm to celebrate closing the loan on her new home in her new life. A life where she did not plan to blend in with the curtains anymore. A life where she planned to stand up and shout, "I'm Emmaline!"

But now, flames licked up the inside of the dumpster as though they were starving and the metal came coated in chocolate syrup.

She sighed. Mostly, the fire was her fault for purchasing a knock-off-brand battery-operated-boyfriend that began smoking before things even got good.

Here's the thing: she was the daughter of a firefighter. He had lectured her about how fires start. Never once—*not once!*—had Dad mentioned the peril of knock-off vibrators.

She should've gone brand name.

Emmaline Eaton learned this lesson in the hardest of hard ways.

Light the neighborhood dumpster on fire the first night in her new home in Denver? Check that box right off the list. She was officially the worst at all things decision-making related.

This was not the way she'd planned to make herself stand out.

The neighborhood stayed quiet this close to midnight, and no one was around. Small blessings and all that. The thin mountain air of Denver's summer was sure feeling thick right about then—and not because of the burning garbage fumes, either.

When the "thing" started smoking, she'd panicked. Tossed that pretend lump of a man right in the trash and took that bag to the neighborhood dumpster.

Em had considered putting out the flames quickly, but she couldn't risk anyone digging through the trash to figure out what had started this mess. Because those indicators all pointed directly at her. So it made lots of sense to just let it burn for a minute. Not too long. Just long enough to destroy the evidence.

She'd briefly hoped that maybe no one would connect the dots on this one. They'd find the who-dittily-do and have no idea where it came from.

But then she'd remembered the mail with her name that she'd tossed out in the same bag. *Burn, baby, burn.*

The neighborhood HOA had the foresight to place the dumpster way off at the end of the cul-de-sac with nothing in the direct vicinity but some soaked grass from the sprinklers. Nothing flammable close by—other than the contents. Contents that needed to burn, burn, burn.

Not to worry, she had a plan to eventually put out the

fire where Bob was burning. Bob being the name she'd given her battery-operated boyfriend when she still had hope for his usefulness. Being a responsible adult, she had a fire extinguisher and a hose with her—she'd even turned on the water at the spigot nearby before she came to battle the flames, something Bob couldn't do. Turn her on, that is. She could just get a Roomba and name *him* Bob. Then she'd at least get clean floors.

Next time she bought herself a vibrator, it'd be top of the line, and she'd name it Banks or something even more unique. Something *creative*.

She used to be creative, but that was before the divorce. Before the marriage, really.

Definitely before the current dumpster fire.

Grr.

"Mom?" Fiona, her nine-year-old daughter, called from the porch of their new home. Oh geez, she had apparently woken up.

"I'm here, babycakes," Em replied, not as loud as her daughter, but with enough volume to be heard through the distance that stretched between them.

"Why are you outside?" Fiona asked, sleep still present in her voice.

"Taking out the trash."

"Why's it on fire?" Fiona asked, like this was totally normal and not that big of a deal.

Which was good because it wasn't *that* big of a deal.

"Everything's fine, baby," Em whisper-yelled down the street. She didn't want to wake the neighbors. You know? "Go back inside. I'll be right there."

She would be once she dealt with this whole situation successfully.

Now was the time to stand tall and deal with things. She was going to deal-the-shit out of this situation. Yes, she stood taller. She was not the Em of yesterday who let the world roll right over her. No, she was doing this life thing right and not hiding anymore.

This was her fault. Look at her owning it. Owning all her mistakes.

"Should I call 9-1-1?" Fiona yelled back. "Grandpa always says to dial 9-1-1 if there's a fire."

"No, babycakes, this is like a campfire. We can sing songs and roast marshmallows next time I take out the trash." Lying to her kid? She shouldn't do that.

"Are you going to use the hose soon?" Fiona yelled again, but at least she stayed at the front door. "Or should I find marshmallows?"

"I'll be right back inside soon," Em assured her. "See if you can find the marshmallows I bought at the store."

Please, dear goodness, go inside.

Blessedly, with the promise of midnight marshmallows, her daughter went inside.

Deep breaths, Em. Deep. Breaths.

She hopped from foot to foot like she was a boxer getting ready for the ring instead of a new homeowner ready to put out a fire at precisely the correct moment.

"Oi! The fire brigade is on the way," a man yelled from up the street.

Well, damn.

Hopefully, that fire crew would not include her dad.

Dear God, let it not be my dad. It couldn't be her dad. The universe wouldn't figuratively screw her that hard.

Would fessing up to the situation be an admission of guilt? She should probably talk to an attorney before she made another mistake. Did divorce attorneys handle this type of thing? Accidental arson via vibrator?

She should google the melting point of silicone. That's what she should do. She had a few minutes of time. The average response to this neighborhood was three minutes and twenty-seconds. See? She knew her Denver fire trivia.

"Grab a hose, mate," the guy hollered from down the road.

Was that an accent he had? Sounded sort of British. But not British.

A bit like those Hemsworth boys—the Chris and Liam guys.

Australian!

"I have a hose," she yelled back.

The hose she was prepared to use once the garbage was good and destroyed. Not one moment before.

"Then use it," the man yelled, coming closer.

Nuh uh. Not yet.

"Why aren't you using it?" the man asked, breathless from sprinting up the street and getting closer by the second.

Oh hey, he was a cutie pie.

"Use it," he hollered again.

Ugh. Fine.

She pointed the fire extinguisher at the flames like the good little firefighter's daughter she wished she was, and let it rip.

Well, hey now, this was actually pretty damn fun. Fire extinguishers were powerful.

She got it. Got why her dad and her brothers all enjoyed this. Heck, she should set vibrator fires more often.

The flames died down thanks to the water and white powder burst. She double fisted it, the hose in one hand, extinguisher in the other. Even she wasn't sure how she managed, but it involved her shoulder, some creative movement with her hand, and a bunch of badassery.

She let the hose work on the residual licks of heat as the wailing siren of a fire truck came closer.

"Y'okay?" the Australian accent guy asked, a touch breathy.

She looked at him and really wished she wasn't wearing her Peppa Pig pajamas. The ones that matched her daughter's jammies, which they both thought were super cute.

Because, *ooooh*, this guy was a good-looking one.

He was handsome, and she was single. She glanced at his left hand. No ring.

Gah. Bad. Bad Em. Focus on the issue at hand, not on the cutie pie.

Still, she couldn't deny that this guy was a looker. Messy blond hair, dear-God-blue-eyes, and that freaking accent women all over the country wanted to tuck into a Sprite bottle and savor. He wore a white tank top that stretched tight across some nice muscles, with steamy swirls of tattoo ink all the way down his arms—though he wasn't a gym rat. Pajama pants slung low on his hips, but she didn't glance down past his waist because, about the time the flames started, she'd given up on sex in all forms.

"I'll have a go." He grabbed the hose. "Let me take it a tick."

She let him. Mostly because he said it so cute with that accent of his and she was reconsidering her no sex manifesto.

"What a freaking disaster." She rubbed between her eyebrows with her fingertips while he finished up with the flames. "I'll never live this down."

Even if it wasn't her dad who came on the fire truck, he'd hear about it and then the holidays would never be the same. Thankfully, her brothers didn't work at the fire station for her neighborhood. Yep, that'd been the requirement she gave the real estate agent when she'd begun her search.

This wasn't her dad's usual station, either.

Also, a requirement. But he floated between stations as one of the Division Chiefs so one could really never know.

"Y'did this?" Hot Blond Guy asked, still spraying the water into the dumpster even though the flames were gone.

She nodded. Willed her pulse to calm down a little. "Not on purpose."

"I've started a load of fires," he said, still spraying away. "Never intentional, either."

This was sweet—the whole hey-I-also-start-fires schtick. And the way he said *never* like *nev-ah*. Freaking adorbs.

Wait a second. Was he flirting with her?

She slipped her glance to him and, oh yeah. He was checking her out.

Her cheeks heated at the blatant perusal.

"I'm sorry to interrupt your night," she said it, she meant it. "Which house is yours?"

"The blue one up the street." He tilted his chin in the direction he'd come.

What were the odds she could convince him never to say anything, ever, about what happened at the dumpster there that night?

"You should probably go back to your girlfriend." Was she fishing for personal details? Yes, yes, she was.

"No girlfriend, I'm afraid." His grin could've melted those piggy jammies right off her body. "Not at the moment."

The way he said that? Implied…oh, she'd been out of the dating game for a helluva long time, but even she remembered how it felt to do this dance with a new potential, someone special.

Gah. This guy probably stole the show wherever he went.

Why did he have to be cute? Why couldn't he be mediocre? Then she could totally flirt right on back.

Sirens up the street wailed, and her face heated. They were coming for her.

"Okay, so here's the deal." She took in a deep breath of air. "I am something of fire department royalty in Denver."

He looked at her like she'd lit the entire street on fire. Not just the dumpster. "You're what? Like a flames princess?"

"My family. They're all firefighters. This has the potential to be very…familial."

"And you keep 'em in business then, aye?" he asked with a tilted grin fit for the handsomest of handsome cartoon heroes.

She sighed internally, but kept her expression neutral. At least she hoped it stayed neutral.

"Not usually. Just moved back." She slid her gaze to her petite house that was perfect for her little family. "And I'd be very grateful if they didn't know this is my fault. I'll never live it down."

"Gotcha," he said. "Family trouble is special trouble."

While that nugget settled between them, things got busy super quick as the fire crew arrived to do their thing, even though the fire was already out. Seriously. Why they needed to hoist around those gigantic axe things? She didn't know.

Thankfully, her dad was not among the crew.

Unfortunately, her oldest brother—James—stepped from the truck with a big ol' axe.

Damn. Damn. Dammit. Damn.

The other firefighters sallied forth, but James paused when he glimpsed Emmaline.

"Uncle James!" Fiona shouted, marshmallows in hand, running toward them in her matching Peppa Pig pajamas.

"Fiona?" he asked, his face screwing up with many questions. "What are you doing up so late?"

"Bringing the marshmallows for the fire," Fiona responded, eyes bright, holding up the big ol' bag of marshmallows. Then she took in the lack of flames and her expression fell.

"Fire's out," Em said, refusing to look at anyone but her daughter. "Head on home and we'll have marshmallows when I get back." They could roast them over a candle or something.

Though, that might not be the best idea. One fire a night already seemed like too much.

James evidenced this by clearing his throat.

She scowled and ensured Fiona made it back to the house, a marshmallow bag dropping in her little hand.

"You can have two before I get there," Em said, loud enough for her daughter to hear.

That got the pep back in the munchkin's step.

Motherhood could be awesome sometimes.

"Em?" James asked in that big brother's voice that was not awesome.

She glowered at him. "What are you doing here, anyway?"

He glanced at the smoldering dumpster, eyebrows raised. "This is my literal job."

"I mean *here*." She pointed to the asphalt. "This isn't your station," she clarified.

He shook his head like he always did when he didn't want to answer her. An outright, not-worth-the-time dismissal.

That. Sucked.

She may as well have disappeared into the dark of night. Unnecessary, and all—

"Em, tell me you did not start this," James said, with substantially more criticism in his tone than was entirely necessary.

Oh, *now* he looked at her like she existed.

"Knock it off, James." His assumption got her hackles raised right up. "It's not like I'm a serial arsonist."

He guffawed.

Only a few times before had she accidentally lit fires, and all of those times she'd been much younger. Not one of them involved sex toys.

"Not her fault, mate," Hot Blond Guy said with that really yummy accent. He pointed to himself. "My bad."

"Your bad?" James raised his eyebrows toward the guy.

This guy was so nice. Too bad he was so handsome, and probably so good at upstaging everyone in his vicinity.

"Yeah, the fire's my bad." Hot Blond Guy lifted his hand. "Name's Ethan."

Did Ethan just take responsibility? Yes, yes, he did. Her mouth fell open the slightest bit.

"Ethan," James confirmed, shaking the wonderful man's hand.

She was going to make Ethan Rice Krispies Treats— her personal specialty. James, however, had practically called her a serial arsonist, so he was getting Miralax in his treats. *Don't eat the ones with the pink wrappers! Ha.*

James did that thing again. The one where he seemed to forget she existed because his entire focus turned to Ethan. Yeah, this was the problem with charisma-soaked hotties.

"James," one of the other firefighter guys called. "Check this out."

As her brother walked away, she seriously hoped they

found a crapload of drugs that would distract everyone from the real culprit.

Grab your copy of It Doesn't Have to Be This Hard today!
Copyright © 2023 Christina Hovland
All rights reserved.

**Turn the page for chapter one of
Played by the Rockstar!**

**He's a rock star.
She's a waitress.
He's about to rock her world.**

Certified behavioral counselor (and former band groupie) Becca Forrester needs a break. Taking a leave of absence from her job, she moves into the apartment over her parents' garage, and clinches a gig waitressing at a dive bar known for bringing in big name musicians.

Cedric "Linx" Lincoln is a certified rock star. Bassist for the hugely popular rock band, Dimefront, he's in Denver while the band is on hiatus a-freaking-gain. He's looking for something—anything—to keep him occupied until they can all get back to making music. When he saunters into his friend's bar, he finds the perfect diversion.

Becca's presence is a breath of fresh air. The sizzle she ignites in him is precisely what he needs. Bonus: no-stress, no-strings hookups are his specialty. But when things between them tip toward serious, his band implodes, and Becca's leave of absence ends, they're forced to decide what their "real" lives should look like. Maybe there's room for an encore…

Chapter One

Becca

NEON BEER SIGNS totally signaled a new beginning. Sure, a girl might not think it possible, but Rebecca— Becca—Forrester was out to prove they could. The scent of hops and bourbon paired with the blast of music through the speakers and constant hum of life in the background at Brek's Bar in Denver, Colorado. Outside, the snow had turned to a slushy mess. Inside, the bar warmed her like she'd taken a shot of top-shelf whiskey.

Oh yes, this joint was the perfect place for a fresh start that did not involve anyone else or the baggage they dragged along with them.

"Why do you want to wait tables here?" Brek asked, giving a dose of emphasis on *here*. "I'd have thought you'd prefer some place with tablecloths."

Becca laughed. Brek was as biker as biker got—long hair, leather, and an abundance of tattoos. His wife was… not. She was a financial planner, and Becca's friend.

Becca shook her head. She definitely didn't want to

wait tables anywhere else. "I'm looking for the diviest dive I can find."

The idea to wait tables was a complete one-eighty from her recent past as a certified behavioral counselor, but she wouldn't go back. Not yet. Especially not when she was having a perfectly lovely time at the local go-to spot for great music in Denver, hanging with her friends, and harassing Brek into hiring her as a part-time waitress while she took a life break.

"Diviest dive? Well, I guess this is your place." Brek flashed her a smile.

"Exactly." Becca tucked a lock of her thick, brown hair behind her ear, where it belonged but never stayed. "Until I figure out what comes next for me."

"You can live the dream right here with me." Brek patted the bar top like it was a living, breathing thing. Something he adored.

Sigh. Someday she wanted someone to look at her like Brek looked at his wife and his bar top.

Not now. She was on a break from all of that—the relationships, the responsibility, everything—but, someday, the adoration thing would be fun to have, too.

He'd created the perfect dive bar atmosphere—neon lights on the dark wood over the bar with his name lit up in blue. The wood paneling covering the walls was new enough to make the place look well-kept but beat up enough that it didn't look like he had tried too hard. Aesthetically, nothing matched. Yet everything still worked together. The place was definitely Instagram-worthy.

The darkened room hopped in preparation for the band to take the stage. A vibe she loved pulsed through the air. That feeling right before music blasts and the lights come to life. Yep. This was exactly what she wanted for her present life: loud music and the familiar faces of the bar's regulars, with no further obligation for the mental or physical well-being for those around her.

Also, the best bands played at Brek's Bar. Sometimes, because he had the connections, Brek brought in huge names. Like *huuuge*. Waiting tables here was perfect for a recovering groupie on hiatus from life.

"You can start next weekend?" Brek asked.

"Next weekend would be perfection." Becca glanced at her friends, mingling across the room.

Then *Linx* entered Brek's Bar. Becca choked on nothing but air.

Linx. Walked. Through. The. Door.

Bassist for Dimefront. Hot as all hell. Heartbreak in leather pants when he took the stage.

She, on the other hand, was only hot when she wore a sweater. Definitely not heartbreak in any kind of clothing. Unless… Could a woman be heartbreak in yoga pants? She was sure that wasn't possible. She shook the thought from her head as he moved her direction.

Her mouth didn't just go dry; her entire body froze in time.

Tonight, he'd ditched the leather and wore shredded blue jeans instead. Lanky, with ridiculously long dark hair, stubble that was a half day away from being a full beard, and all the charisma of a man who could get tens of thousands of screaming fans on their feet with one chord on his guitar. He scanned the room like he owned the joint.

Brek may have owned the bar, but Linx owned the room.

"Looks like my current assignment is here," Brek said, offhand with a touch of growl.

"Linx is your assignment?" Okay, she tried to resist sliding her gaze back to Linx, but she failed. Every woman in the house got the Linx grin as he continued his slow saunter through the room.

"I'm his babysitter…" Brek said, glowering in Linx's general direction.

Crumpet crap-ola. Her blood seemed a whole lot thicker and her skin a whole lot thinner when he sauntered toward Brek… and her. The blue neon halo was a nice touch. Well done, universe. Well done, indeed.

She sighed because…. Linx.

All eyes were on him. Every woman in the room got a solid eye canoodle as he strutted right up to where she stood across from Brek. His eye canoodle could likely get a girl pregnant. She sucked in a breath and braced for her turn.

Linx moved less than an arms-length away, and her heart stuttered like he'd asked her to remove her panties. Surely, he wouldn't recognize her. It'd been years since they partied in the same circles.

She held her breath because she couldn't take the risk of his scent. Not because she had any special superpowers that involved scented rock stars—that she was aware of— but she knew he smelled amazing. Rock star heaven and concerts and something musky, like oak trees in the rain.

"Do you want me to wait for the drinks, or do you want to send them over when they're done?" Becca asked Brek, ignoring the fact that Linx was right-freaking-there doing some kind of intense handshake thing with him.

"You should definitely wait," Linx said, blasting her out of her knickers with that smile of his.

Yes, she often thought in British slang that she'd picked up one summer on a European Dimefront tour. She really took to their language choices. Refined, but still rather raunchy.

Like her. Rather, who she wanted to be.

She slid her gaze up the length of Linx—long and lithe. Not beefcake, but definitely built. He had more of a runner's build. Muscle and sinew, but not overdone.

He leaned against the bar top, a look of pure happiness on his face. This wasn't a cat's-got-his-cream smile. This was a cat's-about-to-play-with-his-dinner-before-devouring grin.

"Becca, this is Cedric," Brek said, slinging drinks like a pro.

Cedric?

Right. Sure, yes, she knew that was his given name. Cedric Sebastian, wasn't it? Last name was Lincoln, and all the original members of the band took a nickname that had an x at the end. Together, they made a triple-x, which they found hysterical, as pointed out in multiple *Rolling Stone* articles.

"Becca," Linx—er, *Cedric*—stretched her name across his tongue and played it like an instrument.

He held his hand out to her. *What to do? What to do?*

She could touch him. She should touch him. He was expecting her to touch him.

Do something already, Becca.

She was overthinking this way too much. So she gave him a solid handshake.

The way he squeezed her palm was nearly erotic. For no good reason, either. It was just a handshake. He didn't make any lewd gestures or anything.

Still, the bar seemed to zip to a pinprick and focus on Linx.

"Becca is a friend of Velma's." Brek tossed Linx a look like her dad used to give her when he thought she was going to use very poor decision-making skills.

Becca extracted her hand from Linx's grasp. She noted how he kept the touch for as long as she'd allow.

"I like Velma." Linx grabbed a pretzel from the bowl on the bar and flipped it into his mouth.

"I do, too." Brek continued working. "That's why I'm making it clear to you that *Becca* is a friend of *Velma's*. Which means stop looking at her like that."

"Like what?" Linx held up his hands.

"Like you want to make her Denver," Brek said with a growl.

What the heck did that mean?

Linx popped another pretzel into his mouth. Somehow, he chewed, smirked, and smoldered, all at the same time.

"She's not Denver. Denver is Denver. Becca is Becca."

Brek crossed his arms. "You and I need to discuss what you're allowed to do and not do while you're visiting."

Linx held his palm to his heart and wobbled dramatically. "I am offended."

For the record, he didn't sound offended.

"It's not visiting if I bought a house. That makes it my home," Linx said to Brek.

He bought a house in Denver? Huh.

Perhaps Becca wasn't the only one in the midst of reconsidering life choices.

"You *bought* a house in Denver?" Brek asked. "I thought it was a vacation rental."

"It was," Linx said with a shrug.

"The landlord was being a total dick about Gibson, so I made him an offer." Linx did the pretzel thing again.

"Who's Gibson?" Becca asked.

Not that she had any real reason to be part of the conversation, but Linx hadn't asked her to leave.

"His cat," Brek said, arms still crossed.

"He's more than a cat." Now Linx crossed his arms. "So what if I bought one little house so he has a place to live?"

Brek shook his head. "Whatever, man. You do you."

"That's my plan." Linx slid his gaze to Becca. "Unless Becca wants to sit here and have a drink with me? Then we can see what happens."

Linx gave her a charisma-soaked smile.

Ah. There it was, her eye canoodle. She felt that stare deep down in her soul.

Yeah. Total player.

A player who went through sex partners like they were potato chips. This was according to his bandmate, Bax, and general female knowledge when meeting a player of his magnitude.

Back when she'd followed Dimefront concerts she'd had her eye on Linx. Something about him was like a magnet, pulling her in his direction. She had wanted him. Full. Stop.

But Linx was bad news for her. He rocked a total love 'em and leave 'em vibe. The kind that made a girl like Becca—someone who tended to see only the good in people and, therefore, fall for the wrong men—step away. He had just the right amount of baggage for her to want to unpack. And he was exactly the type of guy to pick up those suitcases and leave town right after she committed to the unpacking.

So she kept far away from his wandering gaze, preferring to observe him in his natural rock star habitat, and not let her heart, or body, get involved.

Brek handed a bottle of Coors to Linx.

"I've actually…" Becca jerked her head toward her group of friends. "Got to get back."

"That's a drag." Linx shrugged and gave Becca an extra-long, excessively thorough glance.

She shouldn't have done it. But she did. Yes, she totally canoodled him back.

"Becca?" Brek's voice cut through whatever the heck was going on between the two of them.

Brek had, of course, known Becca during her groupie days. Back then, he'd managed Dimefront and she'd been a Ten, the pet name they called their groupies. The Grateful Dead had Deadheads, Justin Bieber had his Beliebers, and Dimefront had their Tens. She'd spent a summer being Queen of the Tens.

This was not something she shared regularly. With anyone. No one else in her real life knew. Not even her best friends. That summer had been her first attempt at a life vacation. And it'd worked. Lucky for her, Brek didn't, and she was quoting here, "Broadcast shit that wasn't his to tell."

She let out a long breath and turned to Brek. He glanced pointedly to the order he'd prepared.

"Thanks." She snatched the remaining drinks and—and this was the hard part—she walked away without looking back at Linx and his neon halo.

Enjoyed the sample?
Played by the Rockstar is Available Now!

Played by the Rockstar
Copyright © 2021 Christina Hovland
All rights reserved.